ESSENCE OF SPIRITUAL WISDOM
Inspirational Thoughts of Eastern Masters

This collection of quotations arranged thematically is unusual. It represents a broad spectrum of spiritual traditions of the East. The quotations are taken from Eastern masters with dynamic personalities who have inspired and transformed hundreds and thousands of people.

GEMS OF WISDOM

R.K. Jain (Ed.)

ESSENCE OF SPIRITUAL WISDOM
Inspirational Thoughts of Eastern Masters

ESSENCE OF SPIRITUAL WISDOM
Inspirational Thoughts of Western Masters

ESSENCE OF SPIRITUAL WISDOM

Inspirational Thoughts of Eastern Masters

Compiled by
Rupali Segal
Anirudh Vasdev

New Age Books
New Delhi (India)

GEMS OF WISDOM

ESSENCE OF SPIRITUAL WISDOM
Inspirational Thoughts of Eastern Masters

Published by
NEW AGE BOOKS
23, Ansari Road, Daryaganj,
New Delhi-110 002 (India)
E-mail : mlbd@mlbd.com
Website : www.mlbd.com

ISBN: 978-81-7822-450-3 (Series)
ISBN: 978-81-7822-444-5

First Edition: Delhi, 2013

PREFACE

True wisdom is inexpressible as words are seldom sufficient. The vast experience before the wisdom dawns cannot be expressed in a few words. However, some masters have succeeded to some extent in doing so, resulting in quotations which capture the essence of wisdom.

This collection of quotations arranged thematically is unusual. It represents a broad spectrum of spiritual traditions of the East. The quotations are taken from Eastern masters with dynamic personalities who have inspired and transformed hundreds and thousands of people. Right from Buddha to Sivananda, from Zen to Bhagavad Gita, from Mahatma Gandhi to Mother Teresa, the wise words of these sages and texts have trickled down through ages propagating truth and knowledge which are not something one can find in school textbooks or college classrooms. They are within us. The challenge is to realize them.

Readers who may find some quotations too subtle are encouraged in the direction of quiet contemplation and occasional rereading which may bring special rewards. Care has however been taken to select only those quotations which are simple, meaningful and inspiring to the general readers. They will find in them a glimpse of that sublime thought which shall inspire mankind to tread the path of right living for all times to come.

The countless hours spent in libraries, long discussions over the phone and endless meetings in the office of the New Age Books have finally bore the fruits in the form of the present book. Working on it has been a wonderful experience and an exciting journey on the whole.

This handy book will be inspiring for all those who seek to practice the wisdom of the ages in their daily life or who just need a few words of wisdom for solace and succour as it contains enough food for thought and reflection. It will act as a catalyst to realize at least a few of the eternal truths if not all.

We are grateful to the publishers New Age Books for selecting us to compile the quotations. The book would not have seen the light of day without their guidance and encouragement.

Rupali Segal
Anirudh Vasdev

PUBLISHER'S NOTE

We believe that in today's fast and hectic life, we seldom find time to reflect on life's myriad mysteries. But we must set aside some time to consciously cultivate contemplation to understand the purpose of life and, more importantly, ourselves. For this, we may seek wisdom from the lives and teachings of the great masters who have inspired millions with their words of wisdom. We therefore thought that their sayings or quotations should be compiled which would inspire and also enlighten us. To begin with, we have compiled in this book the quotations of the Eastern Masters which capture the essence of spiritual wisdom. They would help us to discover ourselves.

We would like to dedicate this book to all those who have helped us, directly or indirectly. While it's impossible to include the names of everyone, a few people deserve special mention. Rupali, who has always been fond of reading spiritual books since her school days, has compiled the quotations in collaboration with Anirudh keeping in mind their relevance to modern life. Anirudh though still a student has already published a book 'Of Ghosts, Wizards & Other Fantasies'. Both Rupali and Anirudh are young, bright and articulate. We're thankful to them for their labour of love. We're also thankful to Mr RK Jain for his valuable advice and guidance; to Jyotsna for her helpful comments, enthusiasm and for producing this book elegantly; and to Sh. Anandji for his patience and technical skills in printing, designing and formatting.

We're planning a series of books on proverbs. The next book will contain the essence of spiritual wisdom of Western Masters.

CONTENTS

Abundance

You can take as much water from the ocean as you are capable of carrying, but if you don't bother to go down to the shore with a pot you get nothing at all...—*Annamalai Swami*

Giving is the secret of abundance... —*Sivananda*

Abundance is knowing that everything you need has already been supplied... —*Shantidasa*

There is enough in the world for everyone's need; there is not enough for everyone's greed... —*Mohandas Gandhi*

Abundance can be had simply by consciously receiving what already has been given... —*Sufi saying*

Abundance is of God; pour into it and it cannot be filled, pour out of it and it cannot be emptied... —*Shantidasa*

If you approach the ocean with a cup, you can only take away a cupful; if you approach it with a bucket you can take away a bucketful... —*Ramana Maharshi*

When you realize there is nothing lacking, the whole world belongs to you... —*Lao-tzu*

Action

Most of people's activities are valueless, if not downright destructive. Dominated by desire and fear, ceasing to do evil precedes beginning to do good. Hence the need for stopping all activities for a time, to investigate one's urges and their motives... —*Nisargadatta*

Action in itself is neither virtuous nor sinful. The error lies in attributing it to our false individuality, when really it emanates from God. So no action is to be discarded. All actions are to be surrendered to Him... —*Papa Ramdas*

There should be less talk; a preaching point is not a meeting point. What do you do then? Take a broom and clean someone's house. That says enough... —*Mother Teresa*

A man rises or goes down by his own actions; as the builder of a wall, or as digger of a well... —*Hitopadesa*

Action should culminate in wisdom... —*Bhagavad-Gita*

Desire is the prompting of all activity. Desire is the urge. No activity arises in those who have attained all desires... —*Sathya Sai Baba*

Action is nothing but the movement of energy in consciousness, and it inevitably bears its own fruit... —*Yoga Vasistha*

The cause of all actions is desire. A desire crops up in your mind for an object. Then you exert to possess the object. Desire is the motive power that keeps up the continuance of life... —*Sivananda*

The only way we can be freed from the chain of action and reaction is by not caring for the result... —*Paramananda*

The difference between what we do and what we are capable of doing would suffice to solve most of the world's problems... —*Mohandas Gandhi*

Activity simply for the sake of activity doesn't provide the satisfaction it promises... —*Shantidasa*

Your thoughts should agree with your words, and the words should agree with your actions. In this world people think one thing, say another thing, and do something else. This is horrible. This is crookedness... —*Sivananda*

There is no power greater than right action in the present moment... —*Yoga Vasistha*

The world is imprisoned by its own activity...—*Hindu saying*

The result of any action is dependent upon the amount of confidence with which it is done... —*Sathya Sai Baba*

He who sees inaction in action and action in inaction, he is intelligent among men; he is a man of established wisdom and a true performer of all actions... —*Bhagavad-Gita*

If the fruits of action do not affect the person, he is free from action... —*Ramana Maharshi*

Action alone is just that does not harm either party to a dispute... —*Mohandas Gandhi*

Abandon all action and come to Me for shelter...—*Krishna*

Only those who do not need to engage in action are happy; they are perfectly content and self contained, and they experience happiness that extends to all the pores of the body... —*Tripura Rahasya*

The acts of this life are the destiny of the next... —*Hindu saying*

That action that takes you towards God is right, and that action which takes you away from God is wrong... —*Papa Ramdas*

Adversity

Adversity is not undesirable. Because, it is only when you are down and out in life that you can realize its true value... —*Papa Ramdas*

You cannot direct which way the winds of adversity will blow, but you can adjust your sails... —*Shantidasa*

There is nothing, no tragedy too great, no malady so incurable, that we cannot find something to counteract it if we do not forget to go within... —*Paramananda*

Adversity may be used as a stepping stone to better things, or it may be used as an excuse for failure. You can measure your own worth by your reactions to adversity...*J.M. Jussawalla*

Behind every adversity lies a hidden possibility... —*Sufi Saying*

A great man does not lose his self-possession when he is afflicted; the ocean is not made muddy by the falling in of its banks... —*Panchatantra*

Advice

No advice is ever necessary from anywhere...—*Nisargadatta*

Do not advise too much; do the job yourself. This is the only advice you can give to others. Do it and others will follow... —*Jawaharlal Nehru*

Do not scatter advice without the authority born of practical experience... —*Sathya Sai Baba*

Seek information, but not from the unreliable; ask for advice but not from the unwise... —*Mahabharata*

All dependence on another is futile, for what others can give others will take away. Only what is your own at the start will remain your own in the end. Accept no guidance but from within... —*Nisargadatta*

Never bother about other people's opinions. Be humble and you will never be disturbed... —*Mother Teresa*

Ambition

Ambition is a mental condition which compels one to work one's self to death in order to live... —*Anonymous*

Ambition renders the mind restless. If the ambition is not realized, the mind is filled with depression and anxieties. The ambitious man has no peace of mind... —*Sivananda*

When you find God within you, all your ambitions are fulfilled...there is no fulfillment of your ambitions for external things... —*Papa Ramdas*

When men's hearts are free from the ambition of earthly power...the light of God shining in them will surely dispel the clouds and create an atmosphere of peace and goodwill... —*Papa Ramdas*

No ambition is spiritual. All ambitions are for the sake of the "I am." If you want to make real progress you must give up the idea of personal attainment. The ambitions of so-called spiritual teachers are preposterous... —*Nisargadatta*

Ambition to earn fame in the world, to gain some position of authority over fellow-men, to lead a luxurious life—this can never insure Mental Peace. Mental Peace is the result of quite different attainments... —*Sathya Sai Baba*

Anger

The wise conquer by strength, rather than anger. The malevolent fall by their own rage... —*Tibetan saying*

Anger seeks to separate rather than join, to tear down rather than build up, to gain an advantage rather than to share... —*Shantidasa*

Your anger is nothing more than your anger toward yourself... —*Ram Dass*

You will not be punished for your anger, you will be punished by your anger...Let a man overcome anger by love... —*Gautama Buddha*

Angry people are insecure people. Anger becomes a face-saving device to cover up deficiencies of another sort. Don't be fooled by the domineering character of an angry person. Know that during moments of anger there dwells a poor self-image... —*Shantidasa*

God turns his back on those who quarrel among themselves... —*Mohandas Gandhi*

When a man's desire is not gratified and when someone stands in the way of its fulfillment, he gets angry... —*Sivananda*

There is no enemy more vicious than your own anger... —*Sathya Sai Baba*

The best response you can give to anger is silence... —*Shantidasa*

When angry, or afflicted with any negative emotion, take time to be alone with God. Do not talk with people who are angry; they are irrational and cannot be reasoned with. If you or they are angry, it is best to leave and pray... —*Peace Pilgrim*

Human nature is so constituted that if we take absolutely no notice of anger or abuse, the person indulging in it will soon be weary of it and stop... —*Mohandas Gandhi*

A man is not wise until he is able to control his passions.... —*Sufi proverb*

Anger is a brief period of lunacy; the most practical way of dealing with anger is to avoid people when they are angry; the worst possible reaction to anger is to respond with anger... —*Shantidasa*

Anger comes to us because we lose contact with God. When we keep in constant contact with God, there is no room for us to be angry...Anger means lack of love... —*Papa Ramdas*

Sometimes we think that when we are excited and angry we exhibit strength. It is the weak person who yields to these lower emotions... —*Paramananda*

Anger and intolerance are the twin enemies of correct understanding... —*Mohandas Gandhi*

From anger arises delusion; from delusion loss of memory is caused. From loss of memory, the discrimination facility is ruined, and from the ruin of discrimination he perishes...
—*Bhagavad-Gita*

Only the ignorant man becomes angry. The wise man understands... —*Indian proverb*

The angry person is never in the right even when right...
—*Shantidasa*

Anxiety

So long as we believe in our heart of hearts that our capacity is limited and we grow anxious and unhappy, we are lacking in faith. One who truly trusts in God has no right to be anxious about anything... —*Paramananda*

Anxiety looks at things and makes you concerned about, even obsessed, with things that seem impossible. It tries to get you to worry, to brood about your problems and needs. It gets your eyes off God... —*Anonymous*

Anxiety springs from the desire that things should happen as we wish rather than as God wills... —*Anonymous*

No anxiety can change the course of things ordained...
—*Papa Ramdas*

The pursuit of wisdom leads to tranquility, the pursuit of wealth, to anxiety... —*Shantidasa*

Apathy/Inertia

Stagnation is not a desirable state. Through struggle we develop strength... —*Papa Ramdas*

There are only two mistakes one can make along the road to truth: not going all the way, and not starting... —*Gautama Buddha*

Procrastination is just another way of concealing cowardice... —*Shantidasa*

Atheism

A man may believe in all the churches in the world; he may carry in his head all the sacred books ever written; he may baptize himself in all the rivers of the earth–still if he has no perception of God, I would class him with the rank atheist... —*Vivekananda*

Those who deny God are denying themselves and their glory... —*Sathya Sai Baba*

Atheism is the death of hope, the suicide of the soul... —*Anonymous*

The conflict between persons who accept God and deny God and those who declare that God is to be found in this place and those who affirm that he can be found nowhere is never ending... —*Sathya Sai Baba*

Awakening/Awareness

Our true nature does not have to be found; it is present at all times, and we need only abide in its unconditioned awareness... —*A Spiritual Warrior*

A being whose awareness is totally free, who does not cling to anything, is liberated... —*Ram Dass*

Awakening, or enlightenment, or liberation is nothing, absolutely nothing other than perceiving profoundly, deeply, intuitively that what we are–that-witching-is-here-now–is the absolute absence of whatever is imaginable or recognizable...
—*Nisargadatta*

O my blessed beloved, awake! Why do you sleep in ignorance?... —*Kabir*

Awakening cannot take place so long as the idea persists that one is a seeker... —*Ramesh Balsekar*

Life is a series of awakenings... —*Sivananda*

When man awakens, he finds that he is part of the one great Reality and he realizes his union with all things...
—*Paramananda*

Every Awakened man or woman knows that the object of life is to realize God... —*Papa Ramdas*

Beauty

There is but one essence of beauty and that is joy. A truly beautiful person is always joyful... —*Shantidasa*

The concept of beautiful and ugly is an individual concept...
—*Yogi Bhajan*

What is beautiful? Whatever is perceived joyfully is beautiful. Bliss is the essence of beauty.... —*Nisargadatta*

If you look for ugliness, you will find it everywhere. When you look for beauty, you will find that everywhere...
—*Narayana*

Beauty and her twin brother Truth require leisure and self-control for their growth... —*Rabindranath Tagore*

True beauty consists of purity of heart...—*Mohandas Gandhi*

Belief

You must recognize yourself for what you are, not what you believe yourself to be... —*Shantidasa*

Men often become what they believe themselves to be. If I believe I cannot do something, it makes me incapable of doing it. But when I believe I can, then I acquire the ability to do it even if I didn't have it in the beginning...
—*Mohandas Gandhi*

Do not believe in anything simply because you have heard it. Do not believe in traditions because they have been handed down for many generations. Do not believe in anything because it is spoken and rumored by many. Do not believe in anything simply because it is found written in your religious books. Do not believe merely on the authority of your teachers and elders.... —*Gautama Buddha*

Do what you believe in and believe in what you do. All else is a waste of energy and time... —*Nisargadatta*

Why crawl with beliefs when with a little more effort you can soar by knowing?... —*Shantidasa*

To believe in the Tao is easy; to keep the Tao is difficult...
—*Lao-tzu*

I believe in the sun even when it is not shining. It believe in love even when I do not feel it. I believe in God even when He is silent... —*Anonymous*

Body

This body is an instrument or servant of the Soul, and not its prison... —*Sivananda*

So long as you identify yourself as the body, your experience of pain and sorrow will increase day by day... If you take your-

self as the body, it means you have forgotten your true Self...and sorrow results for the one who forgets himself...
—*Nisargadatta*

Don't pay too much attention to the body. If you worry about the well-being of your body, you identify with it more and more. Look upon it as a useful vehicle: maintain it, fuel it properly and repair it if it breaks down, but don't become attached to it... —*Annamalai Swami*

Give the body the attention it deserves, but not more...When you cultivate the attitude that you are the body, the body will demand from you more food, more variety in food, more attention to appearance and physical comfort...
—*Sathya Sai Baba*

The true ascetic does not gratify the body; but he cares well for the body that he may advance the spiritual life. Cared for, it is a better vessel for truth... —*Gautama Buddha*

Everything in this world is transitory and fleeting...No man was ever born who could stop his body from changing constantly. Body is the name of a series of changes...—*Paramanda*

This body is mortal, always gripped by death, but within it dwells the immortal Self... —*The Upanishads*

So long as we are attached to the body and external objects, we shall never know true peace... —*Papa Ramdas*

Do not neglect this body. This is the house of God; take care of it. Only in this body can God be realized...—*Nisargadatta*

The body dies but the spirit is not entombed...—*Dhammapada*

Even as a man puts off his worn-out clothes and puts on new ones, even so the Self casts off old bodies and takes up new ones... —*Bhagavad-Gita*

To identify oneself with the body and yet seek happiness, is like attempting to ford a lake on the back of an alligator...
—*Ramana Maharshi*

How can I, who knows the body to be perishable and the soul to be imperishable, mourn over the separation of body from the soul... —*Mohandas Gandhi*

The body, a perishable cage of flesh and bones, we are identified with it, we cling to it, we love it, we are attached to it...
—*Chidananda*

Identifying ourselves with the body is putting the cart before the horse, that is why we stumble in life...
—*Ramana Maharshi*

Man is divine. But he is not aware of his own divinity. He mistakenly thinks he is this little body. But he is not this body...Man is some thing infinite, immutable and eternal...
—*Sathya Sai Baba*

You are not the body, you are only wearing your body; you are that which activates the body... —*Shantidasa*

Verily, there is no freedom from pleasure and pain for one while he dwells in the body... —*The Upanishads*

The body is a tabernacle in which the transmissible human spirit is carried for a while, a shell for the immortal seed that dwells in it and has created it... —*George Santayana*

This body, which you love so much, is time bound...Treat the body like a visitor or guest which has come and must go... —*Nisargadatta*

Cause & Effect

The one who shares will never be lacking, for his or her storehouse will always be full of love, and will receive abundant love to perpetually replenish it... —*A Spiritual Warrior*

People who spit into the wind are defying the workings of cause and effect... *—Shantidasa*

Not in the heavens above, nor in the farthest reaches of the sea, nor by transporting yourself to the remotest valleys of the mountains, will you be able to hide from the consequences of your own evil actions. Likewise, certain are the blessings growing out of your good actions...

—Gautama Buddha

The law of cause and effect is inexorable and unrelenting. You reap a harvest of suffering, poverty, pain and sorrow, because you have sown the seed of evil in the past. You reap a harvest of plenty and bliss owing to your sowing of seeds of good... *—Sivananda*

Sin does not always bear its painful fruit unto the sinner, here on earth, at once; but circling, it reacts unfailingly, and cuts the sinner's very roots of being; and often it inflicts the consequence upon the children and grand-children too... *—Manu*

Never goes a sin without its due return; and deeds of noble goodness, or dire sin, bear their just fruit, here, in this very life. Never is there escape from consequence, because the Great Judge dwells within each heart... *—Mahabharata*

To treat effect while ignoring cause is not the appropriate remedy for any social malady. Any person of wealth can uplift the poor and downtrodden for a period of time, but genuine healing lies in working with cause, the upliftment of the spirit... *—Anonymous*

There is always a close and intimate relationship between the end we aim at and the means adopted to attain it...

—Jawaharlal Nehru

In this world whatever is gained is gained only by self-effort; where failure is encountered, it is seen that there has been a slackness in self-effort... *—Yoga Vasistha*

Do not blame karma, or anybody else, for what you are. You can undo what has been done, through the exercise of a...determined will... —*Papa Ramdas*

A thought of anger or hatred sends arrows from the mental factory towards the person aimed at, hurts the individual, sets up discord and disharmony in the thought-world, and comes back again to the sender and harms the sender also... —*Sivananda*

He who asks questions cannot avoid the answers... —*Oriental proverb*

There is no place in the universe, no mountain, no sky; no heaven where one does not undergo the consequences of actions performed by oneself... —*Yoga Vasistha*

God is the cause, everything else is the effect... —*Shantidasa*

A wicked man who reproaches a virtuous one is like one who looks up and spits at heaven; the spittle soils not the heaven but comes back and defiles his own person... —*Gautama Buddha*

Change

Only that which is real never changes... —*Shankara*

The wheel of change moves on, and those who were down go up and those who were up go down... —*Jawaharlal Nehru*

Your life is not going to change until you change, and the only way you can really change is to stop changing... —*Anonymous*

All changes are taking place in the universe as willed by the divine. Changes are due to the very fact that this manifestation is not permanent. It is ever-changing. But the Spirit underlying the universe is eternal and changeless...

—Papa Ramdas

Everything is destined to change except God and the spark of God within... *—Peace Pilgrim*

When something seems to change in the world...it is really you that is changing... *—Deepak Chopra*

It's only forms that change, not essence... *—Ram Dass*

In this world everything changes, everything decays. Youth becomes old age, health becomes sickness, beauty becomes disease... *—Muktananda*

He who expects to change the world will be disappointed; he must change his view. When this is done, the tolerance will come, forgiveness will come and there will be nothing he cannot bear... *—Hazrat Inayat Khan*

God will not change the condition of men, until they change what is in themselves... *—Koran*

Only the changeable can be thought of and talked about. The unchangeable can only be realized in silence...

—Nisargadatta

The only thing in life you can really count on is change...

—Anonymous

Truth, as a general rule, is severely resisted by the worldly. It oftentimes advocates an unwanted change and change for many people is an uncomfortable inconvenience. The support of custom, the security of tradition does not enjoy being rattled or placed in jeopardy... *—Shantidasa*

If you do not change direction, you many end up where you are heading... *—Lao-tzu*

You are not here to change the world, the world is here to change you... *—Shantidasa*

Change your mind and change your life... —*Anonymous*

Character

Trifles often uncover a man's character best because with trifles, one is apt to be more easily caught off guard... —*Shantidasa*

If you want success in life, if you want to influence others, if you want to progress well in the spiritual path and if you wish to have God-realization, you must possess an unblemished, spotless character. The quintessence of man is his character... —*Sivananda*

Choices lead to action; action forms habits; habits solidify into character...If character grows out of the spiritual vision of oneness and brotherliness, it will lead us to ultimate union with the infinite... —*Sathya Sai Baba*

Character is like a tree–it will always fall in the direction it leans... —*Shantidasa*

A man may die, but his character remains. His thoughts remain. It is the character that gives real force and power to man. Character is power... —*Sivananda*

If you wish to know the character of a man, confer upon him a little authority... —*Shantidasa*

Character is the sum of what a person has left after losing everything else... —*Shantidasa*

Charity

There is only one way of being charitable to another and that is quietly, with no strings attached... —*Shantidasa*

The charitable man has found the path of salvation. He is like a man who plants a sapling and thereby has shade, the flowers, and the fruit in future years... —*Gautama Buddha*

If you can't feed a hundred people, then feed just one...
—*Mother Teresa*

The poor man's charity is to wish the rich man well...
—*Anonymous*

Charity is patient, is kind, feels no envy, is never perverse or proud or insolent; it has no selfish aims, cannot be provoked, does not brood over an injury; it takes no pleasure in wrong-doing but rejoices over victory of the truth...—*Mother Teresa*

Charity is giving someone bread, not a lecture...
—*Anonymous*

The task of feeding the hungry, quenching the thirsty, clothing the naked and healing the sick shows magnanimity of character. But it must be remembered that such charity is only a temporary measure... —*Shantidasa*

Children

If we could all remain children and not grow up at all, it would be such a happy world... —*Ramana Maharshi*

A child is a reflection of God... —*Nityananda*

Your children are not your children. They are the sons and daughters of Life's longing for itself. They come through you but not from you. And though they are with you yet they belong not to you... —*Kahlil Gibran*

Every child comes with the message that God is not yet discouraged of man... —*Rabindranath Tagore*

So long as one does not become simple like a child, one does not get divine illumination. Forget all the worldly knowledge that you have acquired and become as ignorant as a child, and then you will get the divine wisdom...
—*Ramakrishna*

A child is not your ego, it is not a pet dog in the house, it is not a substitute for love. A child has nothing to do with that. A child is born to you so that you can prepare him to face time unto eternity... —*Yogi Bhajan*

As a child learning to walk falls a thousand times before he can stand, and after that falls again and again until at last he can walk, so are we as little children before God... —*Hazrat Inayat Khan*

After all, what is God? An eternal Child playing an eternal game in the eternal garden... —*Aurobindo Ghose*

Children should grow up in the awareness of the brotherhood of man and the Fatherhood of God...—*Sathya Sai Baba*

Choice

The great tragedy of humankind lies in its apparent freedom of choice. Our choices are endless, but also beyond the ability of most to distinguish between what is correct and what is absurd...In truth, there is no choice but one–to rely upon God to make our choices... —*Shantidasa*

We choose our joys and sorrows long before we experience them... —*Kahlil Gibran*

Life is a series of choices and nobody can stop you from making your choices...People punish themselves by making wrong choices, Constantly, enlightenment is being offered to them, but they refuse to accept it. Therefore, people are being taught by problems that are set before them, since they refuse to make right choices voluntarily... —*Peace Pilgrim*

Life is a series of choices and sometimes your only choice is what your attitude will be... —*Shantidasa*

Life is a perpetual choice between endless pairs of rival ills. Right choice, which will bring most happiness and least pain...is a choice inspired by the Spirit... —*Bhagavan Das*

It is the choices you make that are wrong. To imagine that some little thing—food, sex, power, fame—will make you happy is to deceive yourself... —*Nisargadatta*

Always choose the right thing, for brief is your choice. It is like a moment, but it is also eternity... —*Anonymous*

Conscience

The conscience interprets life honestly and realistically; the same cannot be said about the ego... —*Shantidasa*

I simply want to please my own conscience, which is God... —*Mohandas Gandhi*

In matters of conscience, the law of majority has no place... —*Mohandas Gandhi*

Consciousness

A person is but consciousness. Even if a hundred bodies perish, consciousness does not perish. Consciousness is like space, but it exists as if it is the body. The infinite appears to be divided into infinite parts, with and without form. This is because countless particles of experiences shine within that consciousness...

—*Yoga Vasistha*

There is no world, there are no men, there are no women, there is no sin, and there is no illusion. What we see is nothing but the supreme play of cosmic consciousness...

—*Anonymous*

It is impossible that consciousness can ever come to an end. Hence, there must be rebirth. Otherwise, what happens to the individual soul after it shakes off the physical body? It must exist in a different form of consciousness suited to its further growth into greater fullness... —*Sivananda*

The crisis is in our consciousness, not in the world...

—*J. Krishnamurti*

There is individual consciousness and from there, group consciousness and then we reach universal consciousness. The aim of man is to reach universal consciousness...

—*Yogi Bhajan*

There is only one consciousness, equally distributed everywhere. You, through illusion, give it unequal distribution.

—*Ramana Maharshi*

There can be nothing but consciousness. Tell me any place where there is no consciousness; there is no place beyond consciousness. Or can anyone prove in any manner anything outside consciousness? Consciousness is inescapable...

—*Tripura Rahasya*

God's Garment, Nature, changes hues and forms, moment to moment, tireless, ceaselessly; His Consciousness continues ever the same... —*Sankhya-Yoga*

When games and gratifications quickly cease to satisfy, the pilgrim can make rapid progress in consciousness...

—*Sunyata*

Consciousness means freedom from attachment...You realize that the only thing you have to do is to keep yourself really straight, and then do whatever it is you do...

—*Baba Ram Dass*

The world is painted on your screen of consciousness and is entirely your private world...Once you realize that the world is your own projection, you are free of it... —*Nisargadatta*

All consciousness reacts to recognition favorably...
—*Anonymous*

I shall now state clearly the profound secret...Understand that when the ego dies and the real Self is realized as the One reality, then there remains only that real Self, which is pure Consciousness... —*Ramana Maharshi*

When you have achieved the consciousness that God is in you, with you, for you, that awareness must reshape every thought, word and deed, and make you wish good, speak good, and do good... —*Sathya Sai Baba*

That consciousness perishes at the time of death of the physical body is a childish idea. Consciousness is eternal and it persists beyond death. In man the consciousness is veiled by mind and matter. Therefore, he is not able to realize his essential, divine nature... —*Sivananda*

When a man has true knowledge, he feels everything is filled with consciousness... —*Ramakrishna*

What you appear to be is the outer body: what you are is consciousnesses... —*Nisargadatta*

Contentment

If you remain utterly content, you may easily escape the grasp of harm. Pleasures entwined by desire beget trouble at every step... —*Tibetan saying*

Contentment can never make you idle. It is a Sattvic (pure) virtue that propels man towards God. It gives strength of mind and peace. It checks unnecessary and selfish exertions. It opens the inner eye of man and moves his mind towards divine contemplation... —*Sivananda*

Contentment has the ability to squeeze out of every situation all the good there is to get... —*Shantidasa*

The best way to lead a peaceful life is to be content with the situation in which God places us. We seek changes and the result is we get into a worse hole than the previous one... *—Papa Ramdas*

What is contentment? To renounce all craving for what is not obtained unsought and to be satisfied with what comes unsought, without being elated or depressed ever by them–this is contentment... *—Yoga Vasistha*

Happiness comes out of contentment and contentment always comes out of service... *—Yogi Bhajan*

There is no wealth more satisfying than contentment. Eat your fill; you cannot eat more. If you are forced to eat more, it becomes torture... *—Sathya Sai Baba*

He who has known the contentment of being contented will always be content... *—Lao-tzu*

Riches are not from abundance of worldly goods, but from a contented mind... *—Mohammed*

Courage

Courage is fear that has said its prayers... *—Anonymous*

If you are afraid of water, you cannot cross the river even by boat. If you are afraid of fire, you cannot even cook a meal. For anything to be done, first you must have courage... *—Nityananda*

When there is no adversary, what avails thy courage?... *—Rumi*

A man with outward courage dares to die; A man with inward courage dares to live... *—Lao-tzu*

A man without courage is like a dead man. Life without courage is no life... *—Babaji*

You cannot discover new horizons unless you have the courage to lose sight of the shore... —*Anonymous*

Death

In reality, there is no death because you are not the body. Let the body be there or not be there, your existence is always there; it is eternal... —*Nisargadatta*

Death is the temporary end of a temporary phenomenon... —*Gautama Buddha*

Death as finality or extinction is only a concept of thought, and has no reality. Our spiritual essence will continue to flow with the whole and ever change and evolve. Thus, through the death of form we evolve and find renewal. In form our energy radiates outward, and we relate to this energy vibrating around us; but in death of form, our energy radiates inward as we go back into the center of our essence... —*A Spiritual Warrior*

People so often give up in death and that is a pity. Death is not a tragedy to be feared, but actually it is an opportunity for transformation... —*Sogyal Rinpoche*

No university will teach you how to live so that when the time of dying comes, you can say: "I lived well, I do not need to live again"... —*Nisargadatta*

The dead are indeed happy, having gotten rid of the incubus of the body; the dead do not grieve. Do men fear sleep? No, they court it and prepare for it... —*Ramana Maharshi*

Death is not a deplorable event; it is the journey's end, the owner getting out of the car when the time is up and the goal is reached. It is a consummation, a happy conclusion, or at least it ought to be, if only all are wise enough to treat it as such and be prepared for it... —*Sathya Sai Baba*

Sleep is temporary death. Death is longer sleep. Why should one desire continuance of body shackles? Let the man find out his undying Self and be immortal...

—*Ramana Maharshi*

Death is nothing to fear; the body will go, for it is part of the manifestation, but our spirit is the undying essence of the absolute. There is no non-existence, death is just the miraculous, wonderous release of our spirit into a further journey of enfoldment, an evolution within the realm that is our home...

—*A Spiritual Warrior*

In the democracy of the dead, all men are equal. The poor man is as rich as the richest, and the rich man as poor as the pauper. The creditor loses his usury, and the debtor is acquitted of his obligation. There, the proud man surrenders his dignity; the politician his honors, the worldling his pleasures; the invalid needs no physician; the laborers rests from toil. The wrongs of time are redressed; injustice is expiated, and the irony of fate is refuted...

—*Anonymous*

Do not allow death to disturb you, do not let the demise of flesh be the cause of pain or anguish. It is merely rid-dance of your vehicle, the sloughing off of your clothes....

—*Shantidasa*

Death does not end all. Death does not mean total annihilation. Death does not end the chain or sequence. The working agent, the Soul in the body, does not and cannot die with the death of the body. Man's Soul is immortal. Just as a person lays aside his overcoat, so also he lays aside the physical body at death...

—*Sivananda*

Death is an event whereby the body disappears in one way or another–buried or cremated–and the breath in the body ceases and mingles with the air outside, and consciousness which had trapped itself within a body (and had identified itself with it) is released and becomes the universal consciousness, like a drop of rain water falling in the river...

—*Ramesh Balsekar*

Death is not the end of things. Death can be spoken only of the body. The soul is eternal, undying and indestructible. Every death wrung out by the fire of a lofty ideal liberates the soul into the knowledge of its immortality–a kingdom of absolute peace and bliss... —*Papa Ramdas*

Death is not the final accounting. It is merely a time to take inventory of ourselves... —*Anonymous*

Death is considered to be a traumatic experience, but understand what happens. That which has been born, the knowledge "I Am," will end. That knowledge which was limited by this body will then become unlimited, so what is to be feared?... —*Nisargadatta*

Just as one must learn the art of killing in training for violence, so one must learn the art of dying in the training of non-violence... —*Mohandas Gandhi*

O man, do not be afraid of death at all. Thou art immortal. Death is not the opposite of life. It is only a phase of life. Life flows on ceaselessly. The fruit perishes but the seed is full of life. The seed dies but a huge tree grows out of the seed. The tree perishes but it becomes coal which has rich life. Water disappears but it becomes the invisible steam which contains the seed of new life. The stone disappears but it becomes lime which is full of new life. The physical sheath only is thrown but life persists... —*Sivananda*

If you ask, does a man live beyond death, I answer No, not in any sense comprehensible to the mind of man which itself dies at death, and if you ask, does a man altogether die at death, I answer No, for what dies is what belongs to this world of form and illusion... —*Gautama Buddha*

The end of everything that is born is death...construction must result in destruction of that which is constructed. It is a law of nature that birth ends in death and death leads to birth... —*Sathya Sai Baba*

Dissolution of the body is no more than sleep. Just as a man sleeps and wakes up, so is death and birth. Death is like sleep. Birth is like waking up. Death brings promotion to a new and better life. A man of discrimination and wisdom is not afraid of death. He knows that death is the gate of life. Death to him is no longer a skeleton bearing a sword to cut the thread of life, but rather an angel who has a golden key to unlock for him the door to a wider, fuller and happier existence... —*Sivananda*

Death...Why worry one's head over a thing that is inevitable? Why die before one's death?... —*Mohandas Gandhi*

Death is but a casting-off of old clothes... —*Sathya Sai Baba*

Bodies are like pillowcases. It doesn't matter whether they remain or drop off... —*Ramakrishna*

To be afraid of death is like being afraid of discarding an old worn-out garment... —*Mohandas Gandhi*

Never is the undying Self born nor does it die; never did it come to be nor will it come not to be: Unborn, eternal, everlasting is the primordial Self. It is not slain when the body is slain... —*Bhagavad-Gita*

Whatever state of being one calls to mind at the end upon leaving aside his body, to that very state he attains, always being in that state... —*Tibetan Book of the Dead*

People are afraid to die, because they do not know what is death...the moment you know your real being, you are afraid of nothing. Death gives freedom and power... —*Nisargadatta*

Death: where the changing mist of doubts will vanish at a breath, and the mountain peaks of truth will appear...
—*Rabindranath Tagore*

Men fear death only because death is the ending of sense pleasures...
—*Anonymous*

At the time of death, the mind forgets the existing body and enters into another body. Whether you will it or not, what is designed to happen will certainly happen as ordained by God. Hence, it is advisable to leave all sorrows to God and live in peace...
—*Lakshmana*

Nobody is born or dies at any time; it is the mind that conceives its birth and death and its migration to other bodies and other worlds...
—*Yoga Vasistha*

We only die once and the great mystery is in knowing what it is going to be like. How can we possibly prepare for it? The answer is that death exists within life. Life is just a series of changes. All the little deaths that occur within life are teaching us to let go...
—*Sogyal Rinpoche*

Life and death are one thread, the same line viewed from different sides...
—*Lao-tzu*

Death is common in the world. Everyone in it must one day or other doff the physical part of living. Hence, it is not at all proper to be afraid of it...While the body perishes, the Spirit is immortal. We are here to realize we are the spirit. Body is only a vesture, a mask, or a vehicle, impermanent and transitory...
—*Papa Ramdas*

I regard death as a friend, a valet who helps one off with ones's physical plane overcoat when it is worn out or in any other way no longer usable...
—*George S. Arundale*

There is no suffering for him who has finished his journey, and abandoned grief, who has faced himself on all sides, and thrown off all fetters...
—*Dhammapada*

After death, the soul goes to the next world bearing in mind the subtle impressions of its deeds, and after reaping their harvest returns again to this world of action...

—The Upanishads

Nothing can be accomplished after death in the way of spiritual liberation unless it is at least begun during this life...

—Santon ki Shiksha

A man abandons worn-out clothes and acquires new ones, so when the body is worn out a new one is acquired by the self, who lives within... *—Bhagavad-Gita*

On the day when death will knock at thy door, what will you offer him? I will set before my guest the full vessel of my life. I will never let him go with empty hands...

—Rabindranath Tagore

The body is nothing but a covering over our soul, and when it is gone we are not dead; just as we do not think that we are dead when our coat is worn out, or if someone tears our shirt. The moment when a person dies is the only moment when he feels he is dead. The impression of this dying condition, the hopelessness of the doctor, the sorrow and grief of the family cause this impression. After death, as he recovers from this, he gradually finds himself alive...for the great burden has been removed... *—Hazrat Inayat Khan*

Depression/Despair

The biggest disease today is not leprosy or tuberculosis, but rather the feeling of being unwanted... *—Mother Teresa*

When the thickness of anger is repressed, it thins, spreading out into a cloud of despair... *—Anonymous*

No one can ever gain strength by brooding over his weakness... *—Paramananda*

In separation from God is man's greatest misery...

—Mohandas Gandhi

Misery is not absence of happiness, but limited happiness. For as happiness recedes misery pours in...—*Tripura Rahasya*

Gloom is an epidemic disease. All those who come in contact with gloomy people are immediately affected. A gloomy man should cover his face when he comes out...—*Sivananda*

Depression cannot exist in the presence of God...
—*Shantidasa*

Through depression we not only drag ourselves down but we drag others down with us...One who is melancholy has no right to touch another person's life... —*Paramananda*

A morose, gloomy man cannot attract and influence people. He is an infectious parasite amidst society. He spreads gloom everywhere... —*Shivananda*

The cause of your misery is not in your outer life; it is in you, as your ego. You impose limitations on yourself and then make a vain struggle to transcend them...—*Ramana Maharshi*

Some people are sad because certain things are not present and sadder because other things are present...—*Narayana*

Although others may feel sorry for you, never feel sorry for yourself—it has a deadly effect on spiritual well-being. "Before the eyes can see they must have lost the power to shed tears."... —*Peace Pilgrim*

Desire

When all the desires that surge in the heart are renounced, the mortal becomes immortal. When all the knots that strangle the heart are loosened, the mortal becomes immortal... —*The Upanishads*

The more one yields to desire, the more insatiable it will become... —*Mahabharata*

Desire tells us, each time, "Now get thou this, and then you shall be happy." ...The fact is, desire is a bottomless pit which can never fill up, or like the all-consuming fire which burns the fiercer, the more we feed it... —*Lakshmana Sarma*

All desires can cause you trouble, even spiritual ones...
—*Annamalai Swami*

The lust for comfort, that stealthy thing that enters the house as a guest, then becomes a host, and then a master...
—*Kahlil Gibran*

Do not become attached to the things you like; do not maintain an aversion to the things you dislike. Sorrow, fear and bondage come from likes and dislikes...—*Gautama Buddha*

To identify with any desire keeps you separate from God...
—*Vivekananda*

Man's many desires are like the small metal coins he carries about in his pocket. The more he has, the more they weigh him down... —*Sathya Sai Baba*

Where desire is, there is no bliss; where bliss is, there is no desire... —*Sivananda*

The more you find yourself yielding to desires, the more dominant desire becomes in your life... —*Anonymous*

We cannot see everything as divine because we have got a mind which is obsessed with desires. Desires debar us from the vision of the Divine in each and everything...
—*Papa Ramdas*

Gratification of one desire or one set of desires merely gives rise to another...
—*Ramesh Balsekar*

Desire is the creator; desire is the destroyer...
—*Hari Das Baba*

What makes a man unhappy? When he has a desire and it is not satisfied. It does not matter what the desire is...

—Yogi Bhajan

Love becomes lust the moment you make it a means for the satisfaction of animal needs... *—Mohandas Gandhi*

Desires are innumerable, insatiable and unconquerable. Enjoyment cannot bring satisfaction. It is a mistake to think so. Enjoyment only fans a desire... Enjoyment strengthens, increases and aggravates a desire... *—Sivananda*

Don't think about desires and how to get rid of them. Just be still and quiet and all your doubts and desires will vanish... *—Lakshmana*

Desires go on increasing and burning more fiercely as they are fed...The more you yield to desire, the more dominant it becomes in your life. The more you try to satisfy desire, the more you become captivated and enslaved by it...

—Ramana Maharshi

Man is greater than all the objects of his desire...

—Rabindranath Tagore

Where there is desire there is no fullness... *—Chidananda*

All experiences which loom out of contact with the five senses are the sources of sorrow only. All these desires should be abandoned without reserve... *—Bhagavad-Gita*

Who is the greater conqueror? One who with vast armies invades territories and subdues kingdoms, or one who conquers his own desires, his own senses? He is the greater conqueror who has subdued himself, who has conquered his own desires, subdued his own senses... *—Gautama Buddha*

Attachment is real death. Non-attachment is eternal life. Attachment brings manifold miseries. Non-attachment brings manifold bliss. Attachment contracts the heart. Non-attachment expands the heart ad infinitum... *—Sivananda*

There cannot be self-restraint in the absence of desire...
—Rumi

He who is utterly without desire has a happiness that ages not...
—Santi-deva

All suffering is born of desire...Give up desire for pleasure and you will not know what is pain...Only contentment can make you happy–desires fulfilled breed more desires...
—Nisargadatta

Indulging in one's desires in the hope of transcending them is like attempting to extinguish a fire by pouring kerosene on it...
—Lakshmana

To live for the physical, mental and sensual pleasure is like building a home on quicksand, or trying to cross a stream on the back of a crocodile, believing it to be a tree trunk...
—Sankaracharya

When one renounces selfish desires, his love expands into the farthest region of the universe until he becomes aware of cosmic love...
—Sathya Sai Baba

They who are possessed by desire suffer much and enjoy little, as the ox that drags the cart gets by on a morsel of grass...
—Santi-deva

Most of us die wishing we could live again, so many mistakes committed, so much left undone...
—Nisargadatta

Of all longings and desires none is stronger than sex. Sex as a desire has no equal. Rely upon the Oneness. No one is able to become a follower of the Way if he accepts dualism...
—Gautama Buddha

Know this: the object you crave is perishable and transient in itself. How then can lasting peace be derived from it?...
—Papa Ramdas

Sensual pleasure is tantalizing. There is enchantment only as long as a person does not possess the object. He exerts hard. His mind is full of anxiety. He is under despondency as to whether he will secure the object or not. The moment he is in possession of the object, the charm vanishes. He finds that he is entangled... —*Sivananda*

A full investigation into Truth will extinguish your desires at once, and the extinction of desires will restore your mind to rest... —*Yoga Vasishtha*

When the one thought of God saturates your mind, naturally all other desires will disappear from it...—*Papa Ramdas*

Devil

What people call Satan, the Devil, the Black Forces, etc., is simply ignorance of the true Self... —*Ramana Maharshi*

If you reflect upon the devil long enough, his horns will seem to appear on everyone you meet... —*Anonymous*

What is the demon? Your own mind. It is not outside, this demon is inside; that complicates the battle. You have to go into yourself... —*Chidananda*

Many weapons invented by great teachers of mankind for use against the devil have been taken hold of by the devil himself... —*K.Swaminathan*

Discipline

Not to have control over the senses is like sailing in a rudderless ship, bound to break into pieces on coming in contact with the very first rock... —*Mohandas Gandhi*

Carpenters bend wood; fletchers bend arrows; wise men fashion themselves... —*Gautama Buddha*

Discipline divorced from wisdom is not true discipline, but merely the meaningless following of custom, which is a disguise for ignorance... —*Rabindranath Tagore*

It is not possible to discipline ourselves so effectively if out of touch with the world, as while pursuing the world-life with wisdom... —*Manu*

Self-control confers contentment... —*Samhita*

Common-sense is the fundamental factor in all spiritual disciplines. No rule is an eternal rule. Rules change from place to place, time to time and from one condition to another condition... —*Sivananda*

The disciplined man masters thoughts by stillness and emotions by calmness... —*Lao-tzu*

Strength doesn't come from physical capacity. It comes from an indomitable will... —*Mohandas Gandhi*

Doubt

There is no greater hell than doubts... —*Amar Jyoti*

The intelligence of a doubting person dwindles; wherever he looks, he sees nothing but doubt... —*Nityananda*

Doubting is truly a component of man's worst nature. It clips the wings of joy; it dampens enthusiasm, it tarnishes hope. Such men cannot attain the goal even at the end of a thousand births... —*Sathya Sai Baba*

Doubts arise because of the absence of surrender... —*Ramana Maharshi*

Dreams

Without dreams, the illusion is gone... —*A Spiritual Warrior*

Tens of thousands of forests lie dormant within the dreams of one acorn... —*Anonymous*

Duality

Duality is not real, because reality is the opposite of eternity. Without duality there is no perception... —*Sivananda*

The sense of duality vanishes completely once you realize your identity with God. You and He become one. The drop becomes one with the ocean... —*Papa Ramdas*

The maker fused duality in all; sorrow and joy foremost of all these pairs... —*Manu*

They only who love God with a steadfast mind can cross the ocean of duality, and they who rise above this dualness, they only know God as the One Sole Truth... —*Bhagavad-Gita*

When the Reality is experienced, there is no duality at all... —*Sathya Sai Baba*

In the world duality always exists... —*Nisargadatta*

The world and Reality are negations of each other. They cannot be seen simultaneously... —*Ramana Maharshi*

The mind stream on two rival currents flows, heading to virtue and vice... —*Yogi Bhashya*

The world is made of pairs of opposites; all things occur in pairs of two and two...Two birds of wondrous plumage rest awhile on the curious tree of bodied life; One eats the sweet-sour fruits with eager greed, and suffers many ills in consequence; the other looks on compassionately... —*The Upanishads*

Good and evil; altruism and egotism; both are inherent in each living thing... —*Shankaracharya*

A hair's breadth divides heaven from hell. Both are ever present in us. Now the one prevails, now the other... —*Bhagavan Das*

Negations serve to glorify positives. Thus death glorifies immortality, ignorance glorifies wisdom, misery glorifies bliss, night glorifies dawn... —*Sathya Sai Baba*

Humility is the root of honor, lowliness the foundation of loftiness; the world's weakest overcomes the world's hardest... —*Lao-tzu*

It's as though we have two selves or two natures or two wills with two contrary viewpoints...Your lower self sees you as the center of the universe—your higher self sees you as a cell in the body of humanity... —*Peace Pilgrim*

By passion for the pairs of opposites, by those twin snares of like and dislike, all creatures live bewildered, save some few who, quit of sins, holy in act, informed, freed from the opposites, and fixed in faith, cleave unto God...

—*Bhagavad-Gita*

Good and evil are merely conceptional and relative. What is good for one may be bad for another. There are no fixed standards, but only those set by the mind... —*Papa Ramdas*

Are there two entities in the human body? Yes and No. They seem two, but they become one... —*Paramananda*

Ego/Vanity

The ego is like a crooked tree. If you catch it when it is small, it is easy to tie to a stick and straighten out. If you wait till it has grown big, it is far more difficult to control...

—*Saradamma*

When you are governed by your ego, you are selfish and materialistic, but insofar as you follow the promptings of your higher self, you will see things realistically and find harmony within yourself and others... —*Peace Pilgrim*

The tendency of the ego to be humble is like the tendency of water to flow uphill... —*Anonymous*

The ego is just like a ghost. It has no real form of its own...Identifying oneself with the body and mind results in ignorance of the Self. This is how the ego takes birth. Detaching ourselves and disengaging from the body and the mind results in the death of the ego... —*Annamalai Swami*

The more you prune a plant, the more it grows. So too the more you seek to annihilate the ego, the more it will increase. You should seek the root of the ego and destroy it...
—*Ramana Maharshi*

The ego is like an iceberg. Ninety percent of it is underwater. As we observe it, the submerged begins to move into the light of observation, and melts in the light of awareness...
—*Meher Baba*

In a futile quest for pleasure, the ego resembles a dancing horse on a carousel; around and around the ego travels, up and down on the merry-go-round of life... —*Shantidasa*

To the one devoid of ego, the whole world is a heaven of rest, a realm of peace and a kingdom abounding in all happiness. He who has no ego and has surrendered himself to God is the master of every power and force...
—*Sivananda*

Nothing seems to happen exactly as its ego desires. It is simply the mind clouded over by impure desires, and impervious to wisdom, which stubbornly persists in thinking of "me" and "mine"... —*Gautama Buddha*

The ego-life is not life but death... —*K. Swaminathan*

The ego is like an empty glass that dips itself into the ocean and after emerging filled to the brim, cries out: "This is me!"...
—*Anonymous*

The greed to possess things that you see is caused by egotism. Love all things as expression of God's glory, but do not delude yourself into the belief that possessing them will make you happy... —*Sathya Sai Baba*

Think of a vast ocean filled with water on all sides. A jar is immersed in it. There is water both inside and outside the jar; but the water does not become one unless the jar is broken...What is the jar? It is I-consciousness–the ego. When the I disappears, what is, remains... —*Ramakrishna*

Our limited self is the wall separating us from the self of God...It is being dead to self that is the recognition of God... —*Hazrat Inayat Khan*

All suffering surely revolves around egotism and egotism is the sole cause of mental distress... —*Yoga Vasistha*

It is the ego that is the great bar to spiritual progress. If you want ego, then you can't have God. If you want God, then you must be crowned with humility... —*Paramananda*

All unhappiness is due to the ego. With it comes all your trouble. If you would deny the ego and scorch it by ignoring it you would be free... —*Ramana Maharshi*

Men are just like animals so long as they are subject to the ego... —*The Upanishads*

The ego, the lower nature, is of persistent character. It struggles fiercely not to die. The ego lives by denying what is real, conveniently ignoring truth in the process...

—*Shantidasa*

The ego is simply the ignorance that limits the real Self to a single body out of a multitude of bodies, all of which are its own creation...We need to realize in all its implications the fact that the ego itself is the source of all the evil that besets life... —*Lakshmana Sarma*

The only thing which a man must renounce if he wishes to attain the Supreme Truth is the notion of individuality–nothing else...A man who is entirely free from the ego-sense is the happiest man in the world. Because, he has found God–absolute existence, consciousness and bliss–in place of the ego... —*Papa Ramdas*

Praising an egotist is like pouring water on a drowning man... —*Anonymous*

Egoism makes one see glory in petty achievements, happiness in trivial acquisitions, joy in temporary authority over others. But, the Immortal in him is awaiting discovery to confer bliss and liberation from birth and death... —*Sathya Sai Baba*

One of the ego's favorite paths of resistance is to fill you with doubt... —*Ram Dass*

It is characteristic of the ego that is takes all that is unimportant as important and all that is important as unimportant... —*Meher Baba*

When the ego fights, God must go; when God fights, the ego must go... -*Ramakrishnananda*

God is nearer to you than anything else, yet because of the screen of egotism you cannot see him... —*Ramakrishna*

Many could forego heavy meals, a full wardrobe, a fine house...it is the ego they cannot forego... —*Mohandas Gandhi*

Truth cannot be achieved or possessed by the ego... —*Sunyata*

Ego is another synonym for limitation... —*Anonymous*

Ego is only an illusion caused by your ignorance. The ignorance is removed by Self-enquiry... —*Papa Ramdas*

Emotions

Most relate to the world by their emotions, which means they know only the unreality of illusion—this world of emotion is the world of duality, of love and hate, of joy and sorrow. All emotions last only as long as the supporting thought is maintained... —*A Spiritual Warrior*

Emotions are like waves. Watch them come and go on the vast ocean of existence... —*Hindu proverb*

We become our own enemy when we are thrown out of balance by anger, hatred, grief or any other intense emotion. We are for the time being obsessed by something alien... —*Paramananda*

When negative emotions are running high, one rarely makes the best decisions... —*Anonymous*

In the march towards Truth, anger, selfishness, hatred, naturally give way, for otherwise Truth would be impossible to attain. A man who is swayed by negative emotions may have good enough intentions, may be truthful in word, but we will never find the truth... —*Mohandas Gandhi*

It is difficult for an appeal to the mind and the intellect to go far. Most people unfortunately do not think. They feel and act according to their feelings... —*Jawaharlal Nehru*

The man who is involved in the surface phenomena of life is mainly a creature caught up in the constantly changing emotions of life... —*Papa Ramdas*

Enemy

No one will attack a person unless he appears to be an enemy... —*Lao-tzu*

Why should we love our enemies? Our enemy is our greatest friend. Those who speak ill of me, exposing my weakness, do me the greatest good... —*Vinobe Bhave*

We live happily indeed, not hating those who hate us. Among men who hate us we dwell free from hatred!... We live happily indeed, though we call nothing our own! We shall live like the bright gods, feeding on happiness! Victory breeds hatred, for the conquered is unhappy. He who has given up victory and defeat, he, the contented, is happy...

—*Gautama Buddha*

Your enemy is your greatest teacher... —*Buddhist saying*

It is the enemy who can truly teach us to practice the virtues of compassion and tolerance...

—*Dalai Lama*

Conquer your mind and your senses. These are your real enemies... —*Sivananda*

When the heart becomes pure, necessarily your enemy must become your friend... —*Papa Ramdas*

Energy

Energy is increased in solitude...If you are filled with the energy of the Self, that energy flows out of you and nourishes everyone in your vicinity. You don't have to direct this power outwards...this energy will flow of its own accord...

—*Annamalia Swami*

When thoughts of concern for the past and of apprehension for the future are dropped, a tremendous energy is freed for use in the present moment...—*A Spiritual Warrior*

The senses are thieves who steal the energy of the Self...

—*Arunagirinatha*

Energy is wasted enormously when one gets angry. The whole nervous system is shattered by an outburst of anger...
—Sivananda

When you have found inner peace, you are in constant contact with the source of universal energy and cannot be tired...You have endless energy... *—Peace Pilgrim*

As energy runs down, there's a loss of order, which is the real meaning of entropy... *—Vilayat I. Khan*

Energy levels are determined by feelings: depression saps energy, enthusiasm creates even more energy...
—Anonymous

Success is speedy for the energetic... *—Pantanjali*

Human energy is low and the Divine Energy is without limit. You are God. You are the Divine Energy. When you do the Divine work, your energy grows... *—Sathya Sai Baba*

Energy is like a muscle; it grows stronger through being used... *—Prabhavananda*

By anger one loses his energy... Anger transmuted into Love becomes an energy so powerful as to move the whole world...
—Sivananda

If anything is to be done, let a man do it, let him attack it vigorously !... *—Gautama Buddha*

In...Silence we find a new energy and a real unity. God's energy becomes ours, allowing us to perform things well...
—Mother Teresa

Enlightenment

Those who really seek the path to Enlightenment dictate terms to their mind. They then proceed with strong determination... *—Gautama Buddha*

Enlightenment is characterized by the pure inner light. This creation emerges from nothing, it dissolves in nothing, its nature is void, it does not exist... —*Yoga Vasistha*

The spirit enlightens whom it chooseth... —*Hindu proverb*

Enlightenment is simply waking up and recognizing the illusion of life for what it is... —*Shantidasa*

You are destined for enlightenment. Cooperate with your destiny, don't go against it, don't thwart it. Allow it to fulfill itself... —*Nisargadatta*

God realization does not begin in a cave, high atop the Himalayas. It begins in the pots and pans of the kitchen. Treat all of your tasks, however small, as opportunities to see God and serve Him... —*Sivananda*

Words are a distraction to enlightenment. Getting rid of conceptual thinking means enlightenment... —*Ramesh Balsekar*

Enlightenment is the highest good. Once you have it, nobody can take it away from you... —*Siddharameshwar*

You may have expected that enlightenment would come ZAP! instantaneous and permanent. This is unlikely. After the first "ah ha" experience, it can be thought of as the thinning of a layer of clouds... —*Ram Dass*

Enlightenment cannot be attained, nor forced. It can only happen...It can appear only when it is given a vacant space to appear in... —*Nisargadatta*

A person who says, "I'm enlightened" probably isn't... —*Ram Dass*

Enthusiasm

Without enthusiasm, every task is difficult... —*Anonymous*

When you are inspired by some great purpose, some extraordinary project, all your thoughts break their bounds. Your mind transcends limitations, your consciousness expands in every direction, and you will find yourself in a new, great and wonderful world... —*Patanjali*

Envy/Jealousy

Envy is the desire to possess something you don't have; jealousy is the fear of losing something you don't possess...
—*Anonymous*

Envy slays itself by its own arrows... —*Anonymous*

Jealousy is like fire; it eats up goodness, just as fire consumes fuel... —*Sivananda*

If you believe that God pervades everything that He has created, you must believe that you cannot enjoy anything that is not given by Him, and seeing that He is the Creator of his numberless children, it follows that you cannot covet anybody's possessions... —*Mohandas K. Gandhi*

Jealousy is another canker that consumes man. It is nothing but petty-mindedness... —*Sivananda*

Evil

Evil does exist, but we do not have to accept it as an inevitable fact of life... —*Paramananda*

One can only think of spoiling others after one has spoiled oneself... —*Ramana Maharshi*

When God is everywhere, how can there be a place for evil? There are changes and they sometimes appear evil. Everything is at work. Only God knows what He is about...
—*Yoga Swami*

We need to realize in all its implications the fact that the ego itself is the source of all the evil that besets life. But to most inquirers the ego is dear as life itself, because they think it is themselves, and do not want to lose it. They would rather suffer all the ills of life than be happy without it...

—*Lakshmana Sarma*

In the eyes of God there is no evil. We suffer because of our ego...What, after all, is right and wrong? That which takes you towards God is right and that which takes you away from God is wrong. There is no question of right and wrong for one who has realized God... —*Papa Ramdas*

Really good and evil are one and the same, and are in our mind. When the mind is tranquil neither good nor evil affects it...We must find we are beyond good and evil...

—*Vivekananda*

Evil is a screen which hides the truth... —*Hindu saying*

Evil is not a reality, but it is an obsession. It has come with the ego. It will disappear alongwith the ego... —*Papa Ramdas*

Evil can never survive, though for a time it may seem to triumph. It is only a question of our endurance and patience...

—*Paramananda*

If an evil person falls in a well, what should be done? Pull him out. Do not think that the bad will always be bad; lead them to the right road... —*Nityananda*

Whatever good you have is all from God. Whatever evil, all is from yourself... —*Koran*

Every evil thought or deed or hatred, or any other thought or reaction if it is controlled, will be laid in our favor. It is not that we lose by thus restraining ourselves; we are gaining infinitely more than we suspect... —*Vivekananda*

The man who has no wound on his hand may touch poison with his hand, for poison cannot affect a man with no open wound. Neither is there evil for the man free of evil...

—*Buddhist saying*

Non-cooperation with evil is as much a duty as cooperation with good... —*Mohandas Gandhi*

The root of evil is attachment which has sprung from the seed called desire–the primal cause of ignorance... —*Papa Ramdas*

We need not reach out to tear down that which is evil because nothing which is contrary to God's laws can endure. All not-good things in the world are transient, containing within themselves the seeds of their own destruction... —*Peace Pilgrim*

People who seek evil in others, find it. This applies to nations as well as individuals... —*Jawaharlal Nehru*

Example

We must be the change we wish to see in the world... —*Mohandas Gandhi*

A rogue is not an eternal rogue. A prostitute is not an eternal prostitute. Put these peope in the company of saints. They will be newly molded and will be transformed into saints with virtuous qualities.... —*Sivananda*

You think absolute consistency is possible; prove it by example. Don't preach what you do not practice... —*Nisargadatta*

A good example is always the best sermon, the most effective teacher... —*Anonymous*

We can only change others through example... —*Peace Pilgrim*

No one can become another, even by following exactly what another is doing... —*Muni Swamy*

Example is always better than precept. Live an ideal life and by doing so, change the heart of others... —*Papa Ramdas*

Failure/Mistake

Do not brood over failures, defects and mistakes. They will weaken your "will"... Just reflect for a while why you have failed in the attempt and try to be careful in the second attempt... *—Sivananda*

It is only when everything, even love, fails, that with a flash, man finds out how vain, how dream-like is this world... *—Vivekananda*

Failure comes only when we forget our ideals and objectives and principles and begin to wander away from the road that leads to their realization.... *—Jawaharlal Nehru*

Failure is not external. It means something is disordered within... *—Paramananda*

The surest recipe for failure is to try to please everyone... *—Anonymous*

Failure generally takes the path of least persistence... *—Anonymous*

We must never forget that disobedience to God's laws brings disaster, although people eventually do learn by their own mistakes... *—Peace Pilgrim*

If you shut your door to all errors, truth will be shut out... *—Rabindranath Tagore*

Mistakes are your best teachers.... *—Sivananda*

A full and candid admission of one's mistakes should make proof against its repetition... *— Mohandas Gandhi*

There is no such thing as failure for people who have done their best... *—Anonymous*

Faith

Faith is a function of the heart. It must be enforced by reason. The two are not antagonistic as some think. The more intense one's faith is, the more it whets one's reason. When faith becomes blind it dies... —*Mohandas Gandhi*

There is no greater God than faith.... —*Nityananda*

If you repeat anything constantly and generate enough faith to believe that what you are saying is correct, your mind will become what you are repeating... —*Annamalai Swami*

In truth, there is no real conflict between faith and reason... —*Lakshmana Sarma*

Faith is acknowledging that you know nothing... —*Anonymous*

Faith is the belief in the unknown. Faith heals, faith creates, faith works wonders, faith moves mountains. Faith is the searchlight for God-finding... —*Sivananda*

Faith is the temple of virtues... —*Amar Jyoti*

Faith is the consciousness of a reservoir too deep for earthly droughts to run dry... —*Anonymous*

A faith that varies with differing conditions of life is no faith at all... —*Anonymous*

Faith can grow only by long cultivation and careful attention... —*Sathya Sai Baba*

Blind faith should be turned into rational faith. Faith without understanding is only blind faith. Devotion is the development of faith. Knowledge is the development of devotion. Faith leads to the final spiritual experience. Whatever a person strongly believes in, that he experiences and becomes... —*Sivananda*

Faith is the bird that sings when the dawn is still dark...
—*Rabindranath Tagore*

God never fails His devotees in the hour of trial. The condition is that there must be a living faith and the utter-most reliance on Him. The test of faith is that having done our duty we must be prepared to welcome whatever He may send—joy as well as sorrow, good luck as well as bad...
—*Mohandas Gandhi*

Logic and cold reason are poor weapons to fight fear distrust. Only faith and generosity can overcome them...
—*Jawaharlal Nehru*

Faith is a rare flower of inestimable value. It must be cultivated in the garden of your heart. It must be watered daily with the water of sincerity. The weeds of doubts and misgivings should be totally eradicated. Then faith will strike deep root, blossom and bear the fruit of devotion quickly...
—*Sivananda*

Faith expressed in action is a sure means of realization...Faith is not blind. It is the willingness to try... —*Nisargadatta*

He who has no faith in himself can never have faith in God...
—*Vivekananda*

Act as if you had faith and in time faith will take hold of you... —*Sufi saying*

I do not pray for success. I ask for faithfulness...
—*Mother Teresa*

In spiritual matters, faith is the very essence. Doubt shakes the foundations of spiritual practices and is therefore to be avoided. Have faith in the wisdom of the ancients; do not pitch your tiny little brain against the intuitions of the saints and their discoveries.... —*Sathya Sai Baba*

Faith is not blind to needs; faith faces reality but sees reality as measured by God, not as measured by man...

—*Anonymous*

Work without faith is like an attempt to reach the bottom of a bottomless pit... —*Mohandas Gandhi*

If faith is lacking, it is because there is too much selfishness, too much concern for personal gain. For faith to be true, it has to be generous and loving. Love and faith go together, they complete each other... —*Mother Teresa*

Faith is the wire that connects you to grace, and over which grace comes streaming from God... —*Anonymous*

The idea of faith is often misunderstood by people, because they associate it with those who are ignorant, uneducated, and who have no power to investigate for themselves. But faith is not blind belief. It is never well-founded until it is based on experience... —*Paramananda*

God is there for them that have faith and not for them who have not... —*Papa Ramdas*

Falsehood

One person speaks a falsehood, a hundred repeat it as fact, and soon it becomes a truth... —*Shantidasa*

It is falsehood and illusion that always make one suffer–never the truth... —*Anonymous*

Overcome falsehood with truth... —*Peace Pilgrim*

Once you see the false as false, it is not necessary any further to seek the truth... —*Nisargadatta*

Fame

We all want to be famous people, and the moment we want to be something we are no longer free....— *J. Krishnamurti*

Fate/Destiny

By cultivating free will, one can conquer fate...
—*Ramana Maharshi*

Fate is only a name for the final result of all our efforts...
—*Sivananda*

When one was born one had no choice, nor does one have a choice when faced with imminent "death". In between birth and death, however, man considers himself the master of his destiny. If only one gave some quiet thought to the matter, one would surely find that almost every significant event in one's life has had an enormous element of "chance" or "coincidence" in it... —*Ramesh Balsekar*

There is a Divine Plan behind everything, and if we allow ourselves to be used by that unseen Force...many things can happen in a mysterious, miraculous way. If we interfere with that Plan by introducing our own plan, the egocentric plan, tension will be created... —*Satchidananda*

Fault-finding

You show respect for another man's opinions by never telling him he is wrong... —*Anonymous*

Be wary of experts—you don't need to be a shoemaker to know that your shoes fit tight... —*Shantidasa*

Correcting oneself is correcting the whole world. The sun is simply bright. It does not correct anyone. Because it shines, the whole world is full of light. Transforming yourself is a means of giving light to the whole world...
—*Ramana Maharshi*

Love in the making sees faults; love in the fulfillment sees none. Seeing faults is like cutting love into pieces, murdering love... —*Papa Ramdas*

Overlook the greatest fault of another, but do not partake of it yourself in the smallest degree...—*Hazrat Inayat Khan*

Never complain about bad environments. Create your own mental world wherever you remain and wherever you go. There are some difficulties and disadvantages wherever you go... God has placed you there to grow quickly...

—*Sivananda*

Every person should have a special cemetery lot in which to bury the faults of friends and loved ones...—*Jawaharlal Nehru*

It is far better to know our weaknesses and failings than to point out those of others... —*Jawaharlal Nehru*

The narrow-minded man thinks and says: "This man is one of us; this one is not, he is a stranger." To the man of noble soul the whole of mankind is but one family...—*Hitopadesa*

Faults, mustard seed small, of others, you see well; your own, as large as a melon, you see not... —*Mahabharata*

Speaks evil of no one... —*Mohammed*

The faults of others we see easily; our own are very difficult to see. Our neighbor's faults we winnow eagerly, as chaff from grain; our own we hide away... —*Dhammapada*

It is the nature of love not to perceive a fault; once there is evidence of finding fault, love has ceased to be...

—*Anonymous*

You yourselves make or mar your lives. Still you are busy blaming and finding fault with everybody in the world for your sufferings. You fail to probe within and remove the seed of discontent which is in your mind.... —*Papa Ramdas*

It is much easier to find fault than to overlook a fault...

—*Anonymous*

Worrying about the faults of others is an unnecessary addition to the worry we have over our own faults...

—*Hazrat Inayat Khan*

The flies seek filth, the bees seek honey. I will shun the habit of the flies and follow that of the bees. I will refrain from finding faults in others and only look for the good which is in them... —*Hindu Vow*

If he who carefully picks holes in the character of others would but expend the same skill upon himself, what could prevent him from breaking through the bonds of ignorance... —*Anonymous*

Fear

Where there is hate there is fear and where there is fear there is hate... —*Papa Ramdas*

Almost all fear is fear of the unknown. Therefore, what's the remedy? To become acquainted with the thing you fear...

—*Peace Pilgrim*

Your greatest gift lies beyond the door named fear...

—*Sufi saying*

Fear exists wherever another exists... —*The Upanishad*

There is nothing so bad and so dangerous in life as fear...

—*Jawaharlal Nehru*

If you do not come face to face with your fears, you will come to find yourself always running away from them...

—*Anonymous*

Forgiveness

Forgiveness is not for the forgiven but for the sake of the forgiver... —*Anonymous*

To be really sorry for one's errors is like opening the door of Heaven... —*Hazrat Inayat Khan*

Forgiveness is the grace that wipes away all thoughts of judgement... —*Shantidasa*

When we forgive others for the wrongs done to us, it is not the human heart that forgives. It is the divine quality revealed in the heart... —*Papa Ramdas*

If you want to see the brave, look at those who can forgive... —*Bhagavad-Gita*

Those who do not forgive others burn the bridge over which they must pass, for everyone has need to be forgiven... —*Anonymous*

Forgiveness is eminently a divine virtue. The moment the forgiving nature enters into your life, depend on it: God has revealed Himself in you... —*Papa Ramdas*

In order to learn forgiveness, man must first learn tolerance... —*Hazrat Inayat Khan*

The best way to get even is to forget... —*Anonymous*

Forgiveness does not originate from a position of weakness, but is a consequence of strength... —*Anonymous*

There is no limit to which you can forgive those who have wronged you... —*Papa Ramdas*

Freedom

You are already free. Only you have to know and realize this truth... —*Sivananda*

Freedom is not a goal, it is the supreme awareness of who you are...Freedom is found once all concepts are thrown away, and one stands alone in the present moment to find the depth of meaning inherent in the their spirit... —*A Spiritual Warrior*

Freedom is not for the timid... —*Vijaya L. Pandit*

The invisible chains are always stronger than the visible ones...
—*Anonymous*

Do you think you are not free? You are free, but you do not know that you are free—and it is your not knowing that you are free that is your limitation and your imprisonment. Realize your freedom and you are free... —*Vilayat I. Khan*

Freedom: there's none unless you know the Self. But if you know the truth, then you are free... —*The Upanishads*

Freedom is freedom from worry. Having realized that you cannot influence results, pay no attention to your desires and fears. Let them come and go... —*Nisargadatta*

At the end of the way is freedom. Till then, patience...
—*Gautama Buddha*

You are only free when you know the truth and care not that other people know that you know... —*Anonymous*

He only has freedom who ideally loves freedom himself and is glad to extend it to others. He who cares to have slaves must chain himself to them. He who builds walls to create exclusion for others, builds walls across his own freedom...
—*Rabindranath Tagore*

Freedom is not worth having if it does not connote freedom to err... —*Mohandas Gandhi*

Anything you strive to hold captive will hold you captive and if you desire freedom you must give freedom...
—*Peace Pilgrim*

Freedom is only an opportunity; it is not in itself a goal. It simply gives you the opportunity to do whatever you want...an opportunity to find a definition for yourself... —*Osho*

A man who is really free never feels harshness; he is never disturbed by outer conditions... —*Paramananda*

Friendship

A friend is one who knows you as you are, understands where you've been, accepts who you've become, and still gently invites you to grow... —*Anonymous*

I have discovered the ultimate goal in life is to be your own best friend—and only after you have befriended yourself, can you become a friend to others... —*Shantidasa*

Friendship inspires and enriches the life of those who come together... —*Vimala Thakar*

It is easy enough to be friendly to one's friends. But to befriend the one who regards himself as your enemy is the quintessence of all religion. The other is merely business... —*Mohandas Gandhi*

If you have just one or two spiritual friends with whom you can share your highest aspirations, you should consider yourself richly blessed... —*Kriyananda*

Bad company is loss, and good company is gain... In company with the wind the dust flies heavenward; if it joins water, it becomes mud and sinks... —*Tulsi Das*

There is no separateness between two genuine friends... —*Nisargadatta*

If you make friends with people who are without character, your own character will tarnish as well... —*Anonymous*

The use of friendship for selfish motive is like mixing bitter poison with sweet rose syrup... —*Hazrat Inayat Khan*

No man is happier on this earth than he who has a friend with whom he can talk, with whom he can live, with whom he can have a friendly chat... —*Hitopadesa*

There is a magnet in your heart that will attract true friends. That magnet is unselfishness, thinking of others first... —*Paramahansa Yogananda*

Wise company will make you also wise; from vicious friends you cannot but gather vice... —*Sufi saying*

You cannot take more from a friendship than you are willing to put back into it... —*Anonymous*

No one is your real friend except your virtues... —*Muni Swamy*

So-called friends are in reality enemies. You will not find in this whole universe a single friend without egotism. Your true friend in need, He who is sincerely attached to you, is God, who lives within your heart... —*Sivananda*

Giving

God loves a cheerful giver. She gives most who gives with you... —*Mother Teresa*

The best thing to give your enemy is forgiveness; to an opponent, tolerance; to a friend, your heart; to your child, a good example; to your father, deference; to your mother, conduct that will make her proud of you; to yourself, respect; to all men, charity... —*Sivananda*

You must give if you want to receive. Let the center of your being be one of giving, giving, giving. You can't give too much, and you will discover you cannot give without receiving... —*Peace Pilgrim*

Be generous, not wasteful; give, not indiscriminately... —*Mahabharata*

Man only keeps that which he gives away... —*Ancient proverb*

Giving begins with an open heart and ends with an open hand... —*Anonymous*

Love gives for the joy of giving, attachment gives for the return that may come... —*Paramananda*

Trees bend low with ripened fruit; clouds hang down with gentle rain; Noble men bow graciously. This is the way of generous things... —*Bhartrihari*

When you give something to your brother, to your sister, you lose nothing. You gain whenever your brother and sister gain because your brother and sister are also your own Self... —*Shantidasa*

We must possess love before we can give... —*Mother Teresa*

Give to the world the best you have and the best will come back to you... —*Anonymous*

If you would take, you must first give... —*Lao-tzu*

If the sun were asked why he is giving light, if he could speak to us, he would answer that it is his nature to do so...We must be like the sun...This is the purpose of life... —*Papa Ramdas*

Goals

No one has attained his goal without action... —*Bhagavad-Gita*

If one sets up fantasy goals, then it follows that they will experience fantasy victories and fantasy defeats, the inevitable pendulum swing within the world of desire...The goal of God is the reality of yourself; you are within God, and God is within you... —*A Spiritual Warrior*

The goal of life is to become one with the Eternal...You cannot reach the goal without leading a righteous life and without possessing a pure heart... —*Sivananda*

If the will knows not what to will, it will not be able to will... —*Lao-tzu*

One does not begin life in emptiness with a goal of constant attainment; nor is life an urn to be continually filled with superfluous goals... —*Shantidasa*

Life is not an end in itself. Your goal is not conformed to this material world in which your body is living. Your goal goes beyond this world of appearances. Your goal is the attainment of Divine Perfection, which is the nature of absolute peace and joy... —*Chidananda*

There is no goal to be reached. There is nothing to be attained. You are the Self. You exist always...
—*Ramana Maharshi*

All human beings, though they may seem to be walking on divergent paths, are all marching to one goal, and that goal is Self-realization... —*Bhagavad-Gita*

The Goal of life is God-realization... —*Sivananda*

The happiest days are found in struggling toward a goal, not in any attainment... —*Anonymous*

God

It is difficult to know why God reveals Himself to some and plays the game of hide-and-seek with others...—*Papa Ramdas*

The description that God is egoless may seem to be a poor one. It conveys no sense to the ego-ridden mind. People want to be told that God dwells somewhere in the sky, in a world of geat splendor, surrounded by wonderful beings...Even to understand that God dwells in their own hearts, men take time... —*Lakshmana Sarma*

There is one thing God cannot do—He cannot separate Himself from the soul... —*Yoga Swami*

If you are simple and truthful, seeing God is easier than anything else in the world... —*Prabhushri*

When the veil is removed, God can be experienced everywhere in full... —*Sathya Sai Baba*

God is a gold wire on which gold beads of His own manifestation are strung... —*Jnaneshwar Maharaj*

God is simple, everything else is complex. Do not seek absolute values in the relative world of Nature...
—*Paramahansa Yogananda*

If you put God first in your life, everything else will fall into place... —*Anonymous*

Let us be Gods and then help others to be Gods...
—*Vivekananda*

Nothing exists save God... —*Sufi saying*

God is very near the simple, innocent, guileless, unselfish, loving child–unconsciously; or, better, supra-consciously...
—*Bhagavan Das*

God is not like a fish or vegetables that you can buy Him for a price... —*Sarada Devi*

He alone grasps God who does not grasp Him. Anyone who understands God does not know Him... —*Hindu saying*

The acceptance of the omnipresence of God leads to a very profound conclusion. You cannot be APART from Him under any circumstances, for otherwise it would mean there are some places where He is not present...which naturally, is absurd... —*Mouni Sadhu*

God alone is good and perfect... —*Anandamayi Ma*

God is man minus his desires... —*Sathya Sai Baba*

The eternal, unchangeable Lord, who is formless and attributeless, who is absolute knowledge and absolute bliss, evolves the whole universe out of Himself, plays with it, and again withdraws it into Himself... —*Srimad Bhagavatam*

We cannot go where God is not, and where God is, all is well... —*Anonymous*

Whoever finds God becomes wholly God; and unto God there is no other God. Where the sun shines, can there be a night?... —*Sufi saying*

Wherever you turn is God's face... —*Mohammed*

God is always here and now; God does not know distance. And if we fail to make contact with God, it is we who have distanced ourselves from God... —*Shantidasa*

Some people treat God like they do a lawyer; they go to Him only when they are in trouble... —*Anonymous*

God is the greatest democrat the world knows, for He leaves us free to make our own choice between good and evil... —*Mohandas Gandhi*

God has created the world in play...It is God Himself who is sporting in the form of man... —*Ramakrishna*

God is the great magician who can, by His touch, transmute even the basest life into a golden consciousness full of His light, power and joy... —*Papa Ramdas*

When asked where God is, people point towards the sky or some far distant region; that is why He is not manifesting Himself. Realize that He is in you, with you, behind you, before you and all around you; and He can be seen and felt everywhere... —*Sathya Sai Baba*

God sleeps in minerals, awakens in plants, walks in animals, and thinks in man... —*Sanskrit saying*

God generates beings and sends them back over and over again, until they return to Him... —*Koran*

God's Will

Not an atom moves except by God's will...—*Ramana Maharshi*

I am like a pencil in (God's) hand. That is all. He does the thinking. He does the writing. The pencil has nothing to do with it. The pencil has only to be allowed to be used...
—Mother Teresa

To understand the workings of God's will, you have to submit yourself to it unreservedly. Then you come to know that everything happens by His will, and for good...*—Papa Ramdas*

There is a divine plan behind everything, and if we allow ourselves to be used by that Unseen Force, as good instruments, many things can happen in a mysterious, miraculous way... *—Satchidananda*

Most of the near perfect actions or performances, and almost all the works of creativity, happen in this state of egolessness, when the tenet "Thy Will be Done" is actually put into practice... *—Ramesh Balsekar*

Do not say, regarding anything, "I am going to do that tomorrow," but only, "If God will" ... *—Koran*

Live in the world like a dead leaf. As a dead leaf is carried by the wind into a house or on the roadside and has no choice of its own, so let the wind of the Divine Will blow you wherever it chooses... *—Ramakrishna*

Divine guidance often comes when the horizon is the blackest... *—Mohandas Gandhi*

Divine Will prevails at all times and under all circumstances. There is no need to tell God your requirements. He knows them Himself and will look after them...*—Ramana Maharshi*

Divine Will is all powerful. God wills, and everything comes into being that very second. Man wills, but it takes a long time for attaining a thing or materialization of the desired object as his will is weak... *—Sivananda*

Holiness consists in doing God's will joyfully...
—*Mother Teresa*

It is perfectly true that everything in the world happens by God's will alone. His power is invincible. To submit to this power means to permit it to work in and through us irresistibly...resistance to the divine will and power means frustration and misery... —*Papa Ramdas*

God's will is always being done, whether we like it or not...
—*Sunyata*

It is for us to make the effort. The result is always in God's hands... —*Mohandas Gandhi*

Complete surrender does imply that you should have no desire of your own, that God's will alone is your will and you have no will of your own... —*Ramana Maharshi*

Golden Rule

The Golden Rule: "Do unto others as you would have others do unto you," often-times creates a conflict. All people are different and respond differently to certain stimuli. One person's delight can be another person's poison...
—*Shantidasa*

Do not do to others what you do not wish done to yourself; and wish for others too what you desire and long for, for yourself–this is the whole of righteousness, heed it well...
—*Mahabharata*

Good

If you see good in people, you radiate a harmonious loving energy which uplifts those who are around you. If you can maintain this habit, this energy will turn into a steady flow of love... —*Annamalai Swami*

If you affirm the positive, the negatives will drop off by themselves... —*Ramana Maharshi*

If is said that good cometh out of evil. This is perfectly true. Every circumstance in life, when viewed from the right angle, proves to be for good. We appreciate the true value of life only when we have tasted the bitterness of the experience which beset it... —*Papa Ramdas*

There is no one good or bad, only your actions have an effect that is equal and opposite. You cannot get away from Newton's third law... —*Yogi Bhajan*

Let no man think lightly of good, saying in his heart, "it will not benefit me." As by the falling of raindrops a jar of water is filled, so the wise man becomes full of good, even though he collects it little by little... —*Gautama Buddha*

You should make an attempt to find good in whatever you see. Whether you see good or bad you must regard it as good... —*Sathya Sai Baba*

One becomes good by good action and bad by bad action... —*The Upanishads*

A self-realized being cannot help benefiting the world. His very existence is the highest good... —*Ramana Mahrashi*

The greatest amount of good we can do in this world lies not in what we say or in the opinions we advance, but in what we are, the atmosphere we carry with us... — *Paramananda*

A man who claims to know what is good for others is dangerous... —*Nisargadatta*

Grace

Grace is not something outside of you. In fact, your very desire for grace is due to grace that is already working in you...Grace is the Self. It is not something to be acquired. All that is necessary is to know its existence...

—*Ramana Maharshi*

Water flows from a higher level to the lower levels. God's grace too is like that. It flows down to those who are bent low with humility... —*Sathya Sai Baba*

The breeze of grace is always blowing on you. You have to open the sails and your boat will move forward..—*Ramakrishna*

The way of grace is mysterious. You struggle for it and you do not get it. Sometimes, without any struggle, you get it. Its working is governed by something beyond all laws. It is not bound by any rules, regulations or conditions...

—*Papa Ramdas*

Most people have many desires which they want to fulfill. But some rare people tell God: "I want nothing. Make me desireless, that is my only desire." Such a one will be a fit instrument to receive grace...The one who will get the most grace is the one who is completely desireless...

—*Annamalai Swami*

If you go near a tree you will get shade; if you go near a fire you will be relieved of coldness; if you go to the river and drink, your thirst will be quenched; if you go near God you will get His grace. If you do not go near and do not receive His grace, is it the fault of God?... —*Kaivalya Navanitam*

The grace is always there for the asking, always in abundance, but is the seeker capable of receiving it?...

—*Nisargadatta*

With blessing everything is possible...—*Rabindranath Tagore*

All that one can do is to prepare oneself to be ready to receive when the time comes... —*Mahadevan*

Grace is the power of Truth that vanquishes untruth...

—*Sufi saying*

Though we can't always see it at the time, if we look upon events with some perspective, we see things always happen for our best interests. We are always being guided in a way better than we know ourselves... —*Satchidananda*

Is it an easy thing to receive the grace of God? One must altogether renounce egotism; one cannot see God as long as one feels, "I am the doer"... —*Ramakrishna*

The amount of grace which one receives is proportional to the degree to which one surrenders. If you surrender completely, then you will receive enough grace to realize the Self... —*Lakshmana*

Grace is a word which is pregnant with so much divine power and glory that it defies definition. In brief, it may be described as, the love and power of God. Such a love is ever pouring on all mankind, nay, on all creation, because this love and power dwells in and permeates all animate and inanimate objects... —*Papa Ramdas*

Like a lighted lamp, God's Grace spreads all round, on all who approach Him and love to be near him; but if you interpose a shade which shuts out the light from you, you have only yourself to blame if Grace does not shine...

—*Sathya Sai Baba*

Grace can only be attained by approaching God with empty hands and an empty heart... —*Anonymous*

God is not partial. His grace is on all, the good and the evil, just as rains fall equally on all places. Whoever tills the land reaps the harvest... —*Turiyananda*

Destiny is the same as grace. Accept life as it comes and you will find it a blessing... —*Nisargadatta*

God's grace never descends upon a man who is a slave to Lust... —*Mohandas Gandhi*

Gratitude

Wise men count their blessings; fools, their problems...
—*Anonymous*

Most people don't realize the good they had until they lose it, and by then it's too late... —*Anonymous*

You thank God for the good things that come to you, but you don't thank him for the things that seem to be bad; that is where you go wrong... —*Ramana Maharshi*

Some people complain because God put thorns on roses, while others praise Him for putting roses among thorns...
—*Anonymous*

Greatness

Those who aspire to greatness must humble themselves...
—*Lao-tzu*

Those who suppress the thought "I am great" by not paying any attention to it...are great. Those who say "I am great" are small people... —*Sivabhoga Saram*

True greatness is to be free of thoughts...—*Ramana Maharshi*

We can do no great things–only small things with great love...
—*Mother Teresa*

What is greatness? Greatness is when you have found out that you are not great, but everything else is...—*Yogi Bhajan*

Pure, clean, void, tranquil, breathless, selfless, endless, undecaying, steadfast, eternal, unborn, independent, he abides in his own greatness... —*The Upanishads*

He is the greatest man who is the servant of all...—*Sivananda*

Most people confuse greatness with power, despite the fact that greatness has nothing to do with power...—*Anonymous*

Grief

The root cause of man's grief and delusion is the identification of the Soul with the body. Fear of death paralyzes him because he is ignorant of the Soul's true nature. The wise perform their duties in the world, cherishing always the knowledge of the Soul's deathlessness... —*Nikhilananda*

Misery is due to the great multitude of discordant thoughts that prevail in the mind. If all the thoughts be replaced by one single thought, there will be no misery...

—*Ramana Maharshi*

The wise man, knowing his true nature, transcends all grief...

—*The Upanishads*

The world is afflicted with death and decay; therefore the wise do not grieve, knowing the terms of the world...

—*Buddhaghosa*

The truly wise mourn neither for the dead nor for the living... —*Bhagavad-Gita*

Why mourn the dead? They are free from bondage. Mourning is the chain forged by the mind to bind itself to the dead... —*Ramana Maharshi*

Death is inevitable to every born individual. Similarly, birth is inevitable to every dead person. Why do you grieve over inevitable happenings?... —*Lakshmana*

Growth

We are all in the process of growth, a continual evolution—some very quickly and pronounced, others more slow and steady, but all are changing, growing and evolving...we are here to share in the blossoming of consciousness...

—A *Spiritual Warrior*

When the fruit grows, the petals drop off themseves...So when divinity in you increases, the weakness of humanity will vanish... —*Ramakrishna*

Growth cannot be had without first death; gain cannot be realized without a corresponding loss. Always must opposites occur together, one rises high that the other might fall... —*Shantidasa*

Habits

All useless habits are wasted expenditures of energy, and... should be dropped quickly and completely...

—*A Spiritual Warrior*

We cannot in a moment, get rid of habits of a lifetime...

—*Mohandas Gandhi*

Building up character is building up of habits. The changing of character is a changing of habits. Habit is second nature. Character is first nature... —*Sivananda*

All habits increase their power by repetition; resentment begets more resentment and love begets even more love...

—*Anonymous*

Happiness

Nearly all mankind is more or less unhappy because nearly all do not know the true Self. Real happiness abides in Self-knowledge alone. All else is fleeting. To know one's Self is to be blissful always... —*Ramana Maharshi*

Man cannot come in contact with God without feeling happiness... —*Paramananda*

The world is a relative place of good and evil. Remember this point at all times. Try to live happily in any place, under any condition. You will become a strong and dynamic personality. This is a great secret... —*Sivananda*

Unless a person is happy, he cannot bestow happiness on others... —*Ramana Maharshi*

Happiness is your nature. It is not wrong to desire it. What is wrong is seeking it outside when it is inside... —*Ramana Maharshi*

Happiness is within us, and it is ours, but we are always superimposing our own inner joy onto something outside and thinking it comes from there... —*Muktananda*

Nothing can make you happier than you are. All search for happiness is misery and leads to more misery. The only happiness worth the name is the natural happiness of conscious being... —*Nisargadatta*

What is your happiness worth when you have to strive and labor for it? True happiness is spontaneous and effortless... —*Nisargadatta*

Happiness is a quality of mind. It is something we possess within...If we do not have it within, nothing outside can give it to us... —*Paramananda*

The only way for a man to be always happy is to submit to God's will and, leaving everything to Him, be content with the condition in which He places him... —*Papa Ramdas*

We have been accustomed to thinking that we have to get something from outside us in order to be happy, but in truth it works the other way: we must learn to contact our inner source of happiness and satisfaction and flow it outward to share with others–not because it is virtuous to do so, but because it really feels good... —*Shakti Gawain*

The happiest place to live in is just inside your income... —*Anonymous*

Why do people worship God? For happiness. Why do people get married? For happiness. Why do people divorce? For happiness. Everything is done in the name of and for happiness. Still there is no happiness... —*Yogi Bhajan*

Your happiness or misery depends on your state of mind and not upon your external conditions or circumstances... —*Papa Ramdas*

Hatred

If you want to see the heroic, look at those who can love in return for hatred... —*Bhagavad-Gita*

Our first duty is not to hates ourselves... —*Vivekananda*

Hate the sin and love the sinner... —*Mohandas Gandhi*

Never in this world can hatred be stilled by hatred; it will be stilled only by non-hatred–this is the law eternal... —*Gautama Buddha*

The pure, unadulterated love of one person can nullify the hatred of millions... —*Mohandas Gandhi*

Hating another is hating oneself, scorning another is but scorning oneself... —*Bhagavad-Gita*

Health

There exists in every person a place that is free from disease, that never feels pain, that cannot age or die. When you go to this place, limitations which all of us accept cease to exist. They are not even entertained as a possibility. This is a place called perfect health... —*Deepak Chopra*

When we begin to trust ourselves more, the body begins to renew itself and becomes healthy and filled with life energy... —*Shakti Gawain*

Ignorance is disease. Realization is health...What is medicine? God's name... —*Papa Ramdas*

It is health which is real wealth and not pieces of gold and silver... *—Mohandas Gandhi*

Man can be certified as healthy only when he is fully conscious of his reality and is gladly striving to reach it... *—Sathya Sai Baba*

Prevention is always preferable to cure... *—Anonymous*

Arise and accept an antidote to ward off old age and death; it is the knowledge that all wealth and prosperity, all pleasures and enjoyments are harmful to us unless devoted to the good of others; they tend only to sicken and enervate our frames... *—Yoga Vasistha*

Heart

Whatever comes from the heart quietly touches every other. *—Anonymous*

If you keep your heart immersed always in the ocean of divine love, your heart is sure to remain ever full to overflowing with the waters of the divine love... *—Ramakrishna*

Do not let the ways of the world dismay your heart... *—Ramayana*

Why do you read many books? It is of no use. The great book is within your heart. Open the pages of this inexhaustible book, the source of all knowledge. You will know everything... *—Sivananda*

When God measures a man, He puts the tape around the heart instead of the head... *—Anonymous*

Hear this: God can only exist in the heart of man, not elsewhere... *—Nisargadatta*

'Heart' is merely another name for the Supreme Spirit, because He is in all hearts...The entire Universe is condensed in the body, and the entire body in the Heart. Thus the Heart is the nucleus of the whole Universe...

—*Ramana Maharshi*

A perfect mind comes from a perfect heart, not the heart known by a doctor's stethoscope but the heart which is the seat of God... —*Mohandas Gandhi*

Open the doors of your heart, so that the Sun may shine through and disinfect the vices therein and illumine its corners... —*Sathya Sai Baba*

When your heart is full of God, naturally there is no other thought in it. That is renunciation–to have no desire for anything in the world... —*Papa Ramdas*

I am seated in the hearts of all... —*Bhagavad-Gita*

Prayer enlarges the heart... —*Mother Teresa*

Only when the heart becomes purified through the practice of spiritual disciplines does a man attain to wisdom...

—*Ramakrishna*

To give one's heart is to give all... —*Mohandas Gandhi*

Though a wealthy man with a large estate has many rooms in which to dwell, he has one favorite sitting room in which he delights in being. The Lord loves to dwell in the chamber of the heart of man... —*Ramakrishna*

The greatness of man does not lie in his vast riches, exalted position, and name and fame, but in the qualities of the heart. If his heart is pure, free, forgiving, compassionate and humble, then he is great... —*Papa Ramdas*

Heaven & Hell

Heaven is a palace with many doors, and each may enter in his own way... —*Hindu saying*

God is in heaven. That heaven is in your heart. You will find Him there. But you have to purify your heart first...
—Sivananda

Hell has three doors: lust, anger and greed...
—Bhagavad-Gita

The existence of heaven or hell, or whatever it is, is on this earth only... *—Nisargadatta*

One's joy is one's heaven and one's sorrow is one's hell...
—Sathya Sai Baba

It is possible for one person to be living in heaven and another in hell and both be living under the same roof...
—Anonymous

You carry heaven and hell with you... *—Ramana Maharshi*

Here & Now

Don't think about the future. Just be here now. Don't think about the past. Just be here now... *—Ram Dass*

We are within a mystery, a dream of the moment, and the epitome of life is to live ever present within it. Our past illusions and fantasies are not relative to the present moment...Here and now is where all the mystery lies hidden... *—A Spiritual Warrior*

Forget the past. Don't brood over it. Don't plan too much for the future. Try to move through the present serenely unaffected. Then you will experience the peace that is ever present... *—Chidananda*

Realization is a moment by moment happening...There is no coming and going, no birth and death, there is only right now and right here. But no one can say what "here" is, or tell you what time is "now"... *—A Spiritual Warrior*

He who thinks to reach God by running away from the world, when and where does he expect to meet him?... We are reaching him here in this very spot, now at this very moment... —*Rabindranath Tagore*

Look to this day! ...For yesterday is but a dream and tomorrow is only a vision, but today well lived makes every yesterday a dream of happiness and tomorrow a vision of hope... —*Kalidasa*

The 'past' is only a memory and the 'future' is only a hope. It is only the 'present', the now, that means anything to us. —*Nisargadatta*

Humility

No one should be our inferior. One who has learned to be inferior will become superior to all... —*Ramana Maharshi*

If you don't know, you are pure. Not knowing is purity. Then you are humble. If you know, you are not pure... —*Yoga Swami*

Humble righteousness is nine-tenths of the Egoless State... —*Lakshmana Sarma*

All streams flow to the ocean because it is lower than they are. Humility gives it its power... —*Lao-tzu*

Humility is the recognition that what you don't know is more than what you do know... —*Anonymous*

It is our emptiness and lowliness that God needs and not our fullness... —*Mother Teresa*

Humility is indeed only another name for non-egotism... —*Bhagavan Das*

The first quality or virtue we have to develop, before we aspire to have God, is humility... You have in fact to unlearn what you have learnt. You must become simple, unsophisticated, and childlike... —*Papa Ramdas*

Every path that leads to the "kingdom of heaven within" must eventually pass through the valley of humility...
—*Anonymous*

Humility is the richest jewel you can wear...—*Paramananda*

Humility in action is universal consciousness...—*Yogi Bhajan*

One who is meek and humble, who regards himself as the lowest of the low can easily swim across the ocean of this world... —*Maharaj C. Singh*

Humility should make the possessor realize that he is as nothing... —*Mohandas Gandhi*

A humble person can walk with kings and keep his or her virtue and talk with the crowds and keep the common touch... —*Anonymous*

True humility is a great force, and although it works with gentleness, yet it never fails to transform...—*Paramananda*

If you cannot be the sun, then be the humble planet...
—*Tibetan Proverb*

Be lowly and humble, only thus can you rise. The lark builds its nest on the ground, but it soars high in the sky...
—*Ramakrishna*

If you are humble, nothing will touch you, neither praise nor disgrace, because you know what you are...
—*Mother Teresa*

Take the lowest place and you shall reach the highest...
—*Milarepa*

Humility is a virtue that subdues the hearts of others. A man of humility is a powerful magnet or lodestone...—*Sivananda*

A humble person is generally well-liked and respected because he or she does not challenge others. When the ego is not attacked, not put on guard, it has a hard time gathering strength to attack another... —*Shantidasa*

Until the ego finally dies, humility alone is good for the spiritual aspirant... —*Ramana Maharshi*

As life unfolds itself to man the first lesson he learns is humility... —*Hazrat Inayat Khan*

The Chinese character for humility is also the Chinese character for emptiness... —*Anonymous*

Man often exults the defeat of another forgetting that, some other time, his own defeat will be the cause of jubilation for others. So, humility in all the conditions of life is the way to enjoy peace... —*Papa Ramdas*

Learn to know all, but keep yourself unknown...
—*Sufi saying*

If thou wouldst become a pilgrim on the path of love the first condition is that thou become as humble as dust and ashes... —*Ansari*

These are a few of the ways we can practice humility: Speak as little as possible of oneself. Mind one's own business. Avoid curiosity. Do not want to manage other people's affairs. Accept contradiction and correction cheerfully. Pass over the mistakes of others. Accept blame when innocent. Yield to the will of others. Accept insults and injuries. Accept being slighted, forgotten and disliked. Be kind and gentle even under provocation. Do not seek to be specially loved and admired. Never stand on one's dignity. Yield in discussion even though one is right. Choose always the hardest...
—*Mother Teresa*

He who humbles himself shall be saved; He who bends shall be made straight; He who empties himself shall be filled... —*Lao-tzu*

The tree laden with fruit always bends low...—*Ramamkrishna*

Hypocrisy

Hypocrisy begins when one is covetous... —*Sivananda*

To have one eye glued on the enchanting pleasures of the flesh, and with the other to expect to see a spark of Eternal Bliss, is not only impossible but the height of hypocrisy... —*Meher Baba*

Hypocrisy is saying one thing and doing another; it is very easy to spot in others and very difficult to find in ourselves... —*Anonymous*

Ignorance

Most ignorance is the direct result of apathy; people don't know because they don't care to know... —*Anonymous*

The characteristic of the ignorant man is that he strives to be other than what he is...To the enlightened one, there is none who is ignorant... —*Yoga Vasistha*

The senses and the mind of man were created out of ignorance. Therefore they move in ignorance and delight in ignorance. They always find joy and peace in falsities. For their nature is ignorance... —*Sivananda*

Ego is only an illusion caused by your ignorance... —*Papa Ramdas*

The root of ignorance is the idea that a person is separate from God...Ignorance conceals the existent knowledge just as weeds cover the surface of a pond. Clean the weeds and you have the water... —*Shirdi Sai Baba*

Only the fool whose mind is deluded by egotism considers himself to be the doer... —*Bhagavad-Gita*

Man is indeed God playing the fool... —*Papa Ramdas*

Better to live alone; with a fool there is no companionship... —*Buddhist saying*

Desire is an offspring of ignorance... —*Sivananda*

You can tell a fool from a wise man when you rebuke him; the fool will rebuke you back, the wise man will quietly love you... —*Anonymous*

Ignorance makes you identify yourself with the body and your entire life is centered in and utilized for the satisfaction of your senses—the offspring of your lower nature. Therefore, rise up and declare that you are immortal spirit full of power, bliss and peace... —*Papa Ramdas*

If a man does not struggle hard to realize God, he remains steeped in ignorance... —*Brahmananda*

A piece of glass and a diamond are alike to the blind, just as falsehood and truth are both the same to the fool... —*Anonymous*

The eternal, blissful and natural state has been smothered by this life of ignorance... —*Ramana Maharshi*

Those who are blind in this world shall be blind in the next... —*Koran*

Being ignorant of his true identity, man has evolved to be his own worst enemy. Observing his outside surroundings, man often perceives it is an illusionary foe. A fierce struggle inevitably ensues and the end may be predicted with absolute certainty: man loses, wounding himself in the process... —*Shantidasa*

Ignorance or delusion...sets us on the belief that this body of ours is real and makes us forget the all-pervading Divine being who is the one and only reality. Living in this ignorance, our sole outlook on life becomes one continued service of this unreal and perishable body... —*Papa Ramdas*

Illusions

Each person is a specialist in fantasizing their own illusory world... —*A Spiritual Warrior*

When one sees that everything exists as an illusion, one can live in a higher sphere than ordinary man...
—*Gautama Buddha*

Our greatest illusion is disillusion. We imagine that we are disillusioned with life, when the truth is that we have not even begun to live... —*Paul Brunton*

This waking life is just a long dream which keeps our attention away from what we really are. If you take the attitude that all the happenings in the world are dream events, your mind becomes tranquil. It is only when you take the dream world to be real that you get agitated...—*Annamalai Swami*

The greatest illusion is the belief that life has nothing to teach you... —*Shantidasa*

Illusion exists only for him whose sight is bound...
—*Sankara*

Truth is simple, but Illusion makes it infinitely intricate. The person is rare who possesses an insatiable longing for Truth; the real allow Illusion to bind them ever more and more...
—*Meher Baba*

We do not exaggerate when we say that life on earth is a mere bubble... —*Mohandas Gandhi*

People who believe in the reality of the world are really no better than people who build dams to catch the water that they see in a mirage... —*Annamalai Swami*

An illusion is nothing but the shadow of God...
—*Anonymous*

The world is an illusion. Why is it unreal? Because none of the knowledge is going to remain permanent, as real knowledge. I had a number of identities; I was a child, I was a boy, I was a teenager, I was a middle-aged man, I was an old man. Like other identities I thought would remain constant, they never remained so. Finally, I became very old...So which identity remained honest with me? —*Nisargadatta*

The phenomenon of life can be compared to a dream, a ghost, an air bubble, a shadow, glittering dew, the flash of lightning–and must be contemplated as such...
—*Gautama Buddha*

Delusion completely overcomes man's sense of right and wrong... —*Srimad Bhagavatam*

Thus shall you think of all this fleeting world: a star at dawn, a bubble in a stream, a flash of lightning on a summer cloud, a flickering lamp, a phantom, a dream... —*Hindu Sutra*

Imagination

People suffer more in imagination than they do in reality...
—*Anonymous*

Imagination has the capability to choose pain and disorder in the same measure as it does goodness and order...
—*Anonymous*

Once you know with abundant certainty that nothing can trouble you but your own imagination, you come to disregard your desires and fears, concepts and ideas, and live by truth alone... —*Nisargadatta*

Imitation

If you live long enough with the lame, you will find yourself walking with a limp... *—Anonymous*

The wise man never imitates any action... *—Bhagavad-Gita*

Don't drop to the level of others. Let them go on eating dung while you just speak the holy name in your heart... *—Kabir*

Mediocrity finds reassurance in conformity... *—Anonymous*

Immortality/Eternity

The power behind every activity of nature and of man is the power of God. To realize this truth is to be immortal... *—The Upanishads*

Journey

If you want to go east, don't go west... *—Ramakrishna*

The path to God is not an easy one. You have to make your mind and intellect absolutely pure... *—Papa Ramdas*

The true path is through the sky and so has no landmarks and no description. All described paths are but tracing on the earth the shadow of one who has gone in the sky...It is a difficult, a heart breaking path. None can tread it to the end who does not want it more than he wants any other thing... *—Krishnaprem*

The last laps of all paths are the same–surrender of the ego... *—Ramana Maharshi*

One can only make progress on the spiritual path if one is prepared to give up all one's attachments... *—Annamalai Swami*

When you go on a pilgrimage, it directs the mind towards God. But remember–God is within... —*Yoga Swami*

There is no such thing as a spiritual journey; what there is, is a spiritual awakening... —*Anonymous*

The spiritual journey is individual, highly personal. It can't be organized or regulated. It isn't true that everybody should follow one path. Listen to your own truth... —*Ram Dass*

Like the sharp edge of a razor, the sages say, is the path. Narrow it is, and difficult to tread... —*The Upanishads*

A tree as big around as you can reach starts with a small seed; a journey of a thousand miles begins with a single step... —*Lao-tzu*

Life is a pilgrimage where man drags his feet along the rough and thorny road...There is no stopping-place in this pilgrimage...When the road ends, and the Goal is gained the pilgrim finds that he has traveled only from himself to himself... —*Sathya Sai Baba*

There is a path to walk on, there is walking being done, but there is no traveler. There are deeds being done, but there is no doer... —*Gautama Buddha*

The spiritual path is one of falling on your face, getting up, brushing yourself off, turning and looking sheepishly at God and then taking the next step... —*Aurobindo*

Two persons may be traveling side by side in the same direction with perhaps even a common destination. Yet both may be marching on variant paths. How is this possible? If one is marching uphill and the other downhill then they are traveling in dissimilar dimensions and are only side by side for a short length of time... —*Shantidasa*

A fool beholds only the beginnings of his works, but a wise man taketh heed to the end... —*Anonymous*

You speak of paths as if you were somewhere and the Self somewhere else and you had to go and attain it. But in fact the Self is here and now and you are it always...
—*Ramana Maharshi*

To take a journey of a thousand miles, you have to begin with the first step from the place where you stand; the romantic description of the journey and the things the body sees on the way and the description of the scenery are of no use unless you lift your foot and take the first step...
—*Vimala Thakar*

If you do not know the way, seek where His footprints are...
—*Rumi*

The magnetic needle always points toward the north, and hence the sailing vessel does not lose her course. So long as the heart of man is directed towards God, he cannot be lost in the ocean of worldliness... —*Ramakrishna*

In order to know what lies on the road ahead, it might be well to question those travelers who are making their way back... —*Anonymous*

One step makes the next one easier; that is the excellence of the spiritual journey. At each step, your strength and confidence increase and you get bigger and bigger instalments of Grace... —*Sathya Sai Baba*

Joy

The world is not a hell. It is all bliss when ego and likes and dislikes die away... —*Sivananda*

Spirit is never somber. Weeping with the afflicted does not help. It may create a point of contact, but it does not bring a remedy. Joy is the antidote for sorrow... —*Paramananda*

Within your own house dwells the treasury of joy; so why do you go begging from door to door?... —*Sufi saying*

The best way to show gratitude to God is to accept everything with joy. A joyful heart is the inevitable result of a heart burning with love... —*Mother Teresa*

Even if you put all the pleasures of the entire world together in one great heap, they say that the ultimate bliss that each individual soul is destined to attain, even one little portion of that bliss, far outweighs the total pleasure that this world is capable of giving... —*Chidananda*

The secret is, discover the fountain of joy within; that is a never-failing, ever full, ever-cool fountain, for it arises from God... —*Sathya Sai Baba*

Joy consumes time more quickly, not so grief. When men are in joy, time passes fast; when they are in grief, it moves slow... —*Sathya Sai Baba*

Joy is very infectious; therefore, be always full of joy... —*Mother Teresa*

Judgement

Virtually all people are a mixture of good and bad. It is very rare to find someone wholly good or wholly bad. If you have to come into contact with a lot of people, try to make yourself aware of their good points and don't dwell on their bad points. —*Annamalai Swami*

Actions will be judged according to intentions...—*Mohammed*

It is wrong, it is sinful, to consider some people lower than ourselves... —*Mohandas Gandhi*

While man judges another from his own moral standpoint, the wise man looks also at the point of view of another... —*Hazrat Inayat Khan*

You may judge a flower or a butterfly by its looks, but not a human being... (Only) fools judge men by their outside... —*Rabindranath Tagore*

To prove yourself right is just another way to prove another person wrong... —*Anonymous*

When you judge people, you have no time to love them... —*Mother Teresa*

It is a sin to call a person a sinner... —*Vivekananda*

Kindness/Gentleness

There is no strength that compares to that of gentleness... —*Anonymous*

One kind word can warm three winter nights... —*Oriental saying*

Kind words can be short and easy to speak but their echoes are truly endless... —*Mother Teresa*

It is nature's kindness that we do not remember past births... —*Mohandas Gandhi*

Kindness is the root of righteousness. Kindness is the enemy of cruelty, harshness, rudeness. It softens the heart. It opens the door to heaven... —*Sivananda*

Gentleness can only come when we think of God's greatness. Because we forget Him, our pride raises its head... —*Papa Ramdas*

He who is kind and courteous to strangers thereby shows himself a citizen of the world... —*Anonymous*

No act of kindness is ever wasted; like a boomerang, kindness eventually finds its way back to its sender... —*Anonymous*

Thoughtfulness, the kindly regard for others, is the beginning of holiness... —*Mother Teresa*

Kindness begets kindness: this is a law that knows no exceptions... —*Papa Ramdas*

In a gentle way you can shake the world...—*Mohandas Gandhi*

Laughter

Life is a joke, but God is laughing with us, not at us...
—*Swami Beyondananda*

He deserves paradise who makes his companions laugh...
—*Koran*

Lesson

That person who has not learned the lesson of saying "no" will remain wretchedly weak throughout life...—*Anonymous*

Real learning comes about when the competitive spirit has ceased...This is true not only of competition with others, but competition with yourself as well... —*J. Krishnamurti*

Life

Life is going forth, death is a returning home... —*Lao-tzu*

The waking life is just a long dream which keeps our attention away from what we really are... —*Annamalai Swami*

Life is a moment-to-moment happening, any attempt to possess it, save it, or store it, is to lose the present moment...
—*A Spiritual Warrior*

In the final analysis, earth-life is a joke. Do not regard it seriously. All your problems stem from seeing life in a solemn manner. One hundred years from now you'll be chuckling at your so-called somberness. Lighten up!...
—*Anonymous*

Life is always forcing us to compromise...—*Jawaharlal Nehru*

Life is no thing or state of a thing, but a continuous movement or change... —*S. Radhakrishnan*

Life is like a game of cards. The hand that is dealt you represents determinism; the way you play it is free will...

—*Jawaharlal Nehru*

Life vibrates. It does not move... —*Vimala Thakar*

Life is more than just trying to get everything; life is learning not to be attached to anything... —*Anonymous*

Life is a journey from impurity to purity, from hatred to cosmic love, from death to immortality, from slavery to freedom, from imperfection to perfection, from pain to eternal bliss, from diversity to unity, from ignorance to eternal wisdom, and from weakness to strength... —*Sivananda*

As you watch it, your life turns to dust... —*Kabir*

Life is a campaign against foes, it is a battle with obstacles, temptations, hardships and limitations. These foes are within man and so the battle has to be incessant and perpetual...

—*Sathya Sai Baba*

The purpose of life is like a horizon; the further one advances, the farther it recedes... —*Hazrat Inayat Khan*

Life would be dull and colorless but for the obstacles that we have to overcome and the fights we have to win...

—*Jawaharlal Nehru*

Life is learning which rules to obey, which rules not to obey, and the wisdom to tell the difference between the two...

—*Anonymous*

The greatest abundance is gained by not falling into the whirlpool of life... —*Lakshmana*

Life wants to give us the best, but you must make application for it, you must work for it in the unseen...—*Anonymous*

Light

A candle never loses anything when it lights another candle...
—*Anonymous*

To keep a lamp burning we have to keep putting oil into it...
—*Mother Teresa*

A man who moves with the earth will necessarily experience days and nights. He who stays with the sun will know no darkness...
—*Nisargadatta*

If you enter a dark place with a lamp, light falls on everyone who is near you. You don't have to tell people, "I have a light" because they will all be aware of its presence...
—*Annamalai Swami*

There is no darkness if you face the sun...
—*Amar Jyoti*

In order to cause a shadow to disappear you must shine a light upon it...
—*Anonymous*

Do you not seek a light, ye who are surrounded in darkness...
—*Dhammapada*

Lead me from the unreal to the real! Lead me from darkness to light...
—*The Upanishads*

Light and darkness cannot exist at the same time. When you bring in light, darkness must fly; no matter what darkness it is, it must fly. So that is the power of light...
—*Chidananda*

In the light there are no mysteries, no hidden things, everything is revealed; only in darkness are things concealed...
—*Anonymous*

It takes only a little light to dispel much darkness...
—*Anonymous*

Little

We ourselves feel that what we are doing is just a drop in the ocean. But if that drop was not in the ocean, I think the ocean would be less because of that missing drop. I do not agree with the big way of doing things... —*Mother Teresa*

The Godly nature does not need to be sated with trivial items and petty praises. Already it contains whatever is needed to sustain itself... —*Shantidasa*

Trivial words or gestures are apt to reveal an individual far more than his studied poses and utterances...
—*Jawaharlal Nehru*

Loneliness

Loneliness and feelings of being unwanted is the most terrible poverty... —*Mother Teresa*

We all have to cross the stream alone... —*Bhai Sahib*

Love

Ordinary love based on the physical affinity is a source of misery both to the lover and the loved. But Divine Love based on the feeling of spiritual oneness is sublime. It is a source of pure bliss. Here you love another not because he is a relation of yours, but because you and he are one in Spirit....
—*Papa Ramdas*

The passion we call love is the misguided belief that one person is somehow different from another person...
—*Anonymous*

Love is the end of the struggle. When you have got love, your struggle ceases... —*Papa Ramdas*

Love of body or skin is passion. Love of God is...devotion. It is pure love. It is love for love's sake. It is divine... —*Sivananda*

Try to radiate your love equally to all people instead of just a few. Try to feel that the whole world is your Self, your God. Try to see the Self in all people. Spread your love in all directions as an act of worship and surrender, because everything in the world is a manifestation of God...

—Annamalai Swami

Love and compassion are necessities, not luxuries. Without them humanity cannot survive... *—Dalai Lama*

The path of love is rugged, thorny and precipitous. It is a razor path...It can only admit one... *—Sivananda*

There is no path greater than love. There is no law higher than love. And there is no goal beyond love. God and love are identical... *—Meher Baba*

You want to be loved because you do not love; but the moment you love, it is finished, you are no longer inquiring whether or not somebody loves you... *—J. Krishnamurti*

Love is the energizing elixir of the universe, the cause and effect of all harmonies... *—Rumi*

As a mother even at the risk of her own life protects her only son, so let a man cultivate goodwill without measure among all beings. Let him suffuse the whole world with thoughts of love, unmixed with any sense of difference or opposed interests... *—Gautama Buddha*

Love is mysterious divine glue that unites the hearts of all...

—Sivananda

Immature love says, "I love you because you love me." Mature love says, "I love you whether you love me or not."...

—Shantidasa

Love is not selective, desire is selective; with love there are no strangers... *—Anonymous*

Love in the making sees faults, but forgives them. Love in its grand fulfillment never sees any faults; hence it has nothing to forgive... *—Papa Ramdas*

Love is the strongest force the world possesses, and yet it is the humblest imaginable... *—Mohandas Gandhi*

To love is the most important thing in life. But what do we mean by love? When you love someone because that person loves you in return surely that is not love. To love is to have that extraordinary feeling of affection without asking anything in return... *—J.Krishnamurti*

Love is clarity...Decisions made from love will bring even greater clarity... *—Maya Sarada Devi*

Love is not bargaining; it is not give and take. It is a spontaneous merging of souls... *—Papa Ramdas*

Start learning to love God by loving those whom you cannot love. The more you remember others with kindness and generosity, the more you forget yourself, and when you forget yourself completely, you find God... *—Meher Baba*

The love in your heart wasn't put there to stay–Love isn't love until it's given away... *—Anonymous*

While God awaits for the temple to be built of love, men bring stones... *—Rabindranath Tagore*

Love is a fruit in season at all times, and within the reach of every hand... *–Mother Teresa*

I am realizing every day that the search for truth is vain unless it is founded upon love. To injure a single human being is to injure those divine powers within us, and thus the harm reaches not only that one human being, but with him the whole world... *—Mohandas Gandhi*

He who comes to do good knocks at the gate; he who loves finds the gate open... *—Rabindranath Tagore*

To love all alike is distinctly a divine quality...—*Papa Ramdas*

Meditation

Keeping God in your mind as everything around you becomes meditation... —*Ramana Maharshi*

Meditation is silence. If you realize that you really know nothing, then you will be truly meditating. Such truthfulness is the right soil for silence. Silence is meditation...—*Yoga Swami*

Meditation needs an awake mind not an unconscious one...Meditation is not something that should be done in a particular position at a particular time. It is an awareness that must persist throughout the day...—*Annamalai Swami*

Meditation is not some strange technique that we have to learn with great effort and difficulty...Whatever we accomplish in this world we accomplish through the power of concentration, which is nothing but meditation...Above all, meditation stills the wandering mind and establishes us forever in a state of peace... —*Muktananda*

This is the only way...to explain existence, to overcome sadness and grievances, to banish death and misery, to find the right path, to realize Nirvana–it is correct meditation...

—*Gautama Buddha*

Before embarking on important undertakings, sit quietly, calm your senses and thoughts, and meditate deeply. You will then be guided by the great creative power of Spirit...

—*Paramahansa Yogananda*

Meditation is not a means to an end. It is both the means and the end... —*J. Krishnamurti*

There is no ill in life that cannot be cured by right meditation....True meditation gives us, as it were, wings for flight to a higher realm and thus detaches us from terrestrial fetters... —*Paramananda*

The mind turned outward results in thoughts and objects. Turned inwards it becomes itself the Self...

—Ramana Maharshi

Meditation applies the brakes to the mind...

—Ramana Maharshi

Some hours of the day should be set apart for meditation so that the work in which we would be engaged during the other hours may be done as a spontaneous and blissful outflow of Eternal Reality dwelling in us... *—Papa Ramdas*

Arise in the midst of the night and commune with thy God. The ego will be crushed and things will be revealed to thee thou didst not know before and thy path in life will be made smooth... *—Koran*

Through meditation, the Higher Self is seen...

—Bhagavad-Gita

There is only one meditation–the rigorous refusal to harbor thoughts. To be free from thoughts is itself meditation...

—Nisargadatta

Do you know what one feels in meditation? The mind becomes like a continuous flow of oil–it thinks one object only, and that is God. It does not think of anything else...

—Ramakrishna

What is meditation? It is the suspension of thoughts...

—Ramana Maharshi

It were better to live one single day in the pursuit of understanding and meditation, than to live a hunderd years in ignorance and restraint... *—Gautama Buddha*

Mind

There is no misery or suffering outside your own mind because the whole world is nothing but a projection of your mind... *—Annamalai Swami*

Mind is only thoughts. The more easily you can be without thoughts, the nearer you are to a direct experience of Self. To make the mind die you must deprive it of thoughts...

—*Lakshmana*

The thoughts within our mind are in our power to control, but few ever exercise their freedom to control them, and instead are witness to an endless parade of fantasy, concepts and illusions... —*A Spiritual Warrior*

The mind is the commander-in-chief and the senses are the armed forces. Hence, control of the mind is control (or victory) over the senses. If one's feet are covered with leather shoes, the entire world is covered with leather...

—*Yoga Vasistha*

There is only one means to control one's mind that is to destroy thoughts as soon as they arise... — The *Upanishads*

Whenever you jettison false notions from the mind you make room for reality to enter... —*Anonymous*

If you give your mind your full, detached attention, you begin to understand the futility of all mental activities. Watch the mind wandering here and there, seeking out useless or unnecessary things or ideas which will ultimately only create misery for itself... —*Annamalai Swami*

One must first discipline and control one's own mind. If a man can control his own mind he will find the way to Enlightenment, and all wisdom and virtue will naturally come to him... —*Gautama Buddha*

The mind is the mischief-maker. It jumps from doubt to doubt; it puts obstacles in the way. It weaves a net and gets entangled in it. It is ever discontented; it runs after a hundred things and away from another hundred...

—*Sathya Sai Baba*

There is nothing wrong with God's creation. Misery and suffering only exist in the mind... —*Ramana Maharshi*

The mind is, without a doubt, unsteady and difficult to curb, but it can be controlled through practice and dispassion... —*Bhagavad-Gita*

If there's no desire in the mind, there's no mind at all. The mind is like a rockpile. Take all the rocks away and there is no pile... —*Satchidananda*

The mind is an instrument for communication, for practical purposes. The mind cannot grasp the truth. The Self witnesses the mind, but the mind cannot catch hold of the Self... The mind can only work with some name or form or image. If you give this up, the mind will be helpless... —*Nisargadatta*

The mind is like a strolling street dog. You are eating out of garbage cans. You who are heir to immortal glory, divine blessedness–why are you picking up these little droppings and trying to fill yourself?... —*Sivananda*

Mind control is not one's birthright. The successful few owe their success to their perseverance... —*Ramana Maharshi*

The "inner voice" is not always reliable, as much depends upon the purity of one's mind... —*Shantidasa*

Man's minds perceive second causes, but only prophets perceive the action of the First Cause... *Rumi*

Every passion, every emotion, has its effect upon the mind. Every change of mind, however slight, has its effect upon the body... —*Hazrat Inayat Khan*

The mind is said to be two-fold: the pure and also the impure; impure by union with desire–pure when from desire completely free... —*The Upanishads*

Mind is consciousness which has put on limitations. You are originally unlimited and perfect. Later you take on limitations and become the mind... —*Ramana Maharshi*

In the sky there is no distinction of east and west; people create distinctions out of their own minds and then believe them to be true.... —*Gautama Buddha*

The mind has a way of being drawn away by passing fancy... The mind is the enchanter, the usurper who has established sovereignty over you... —*Sathya Sai Baba*

Mind is thought. Thought means emotions, hopes, memory. Erase the emotions, good or bad, erase hope and disappointments, erase the memory, and the mind will be stilled... —*Deepa Kodikal*

Chastity is a mind that is completely free from all image-making, all the pictures, sensations, which thought has built in its search for pleasure through sex. Then you will find an abundance of energy... —*J. Krishnamurti*

The mind flows along the course of wisdom or of ignorance, in whatever direction you make it flow... —*Yoga Vasistha*

A tamed mind brings happiness... —*Dhammapada*

Purity of mind and idleness are incompatible... —*Mohandas Gandhi*

Your mind may be likened to an incubator which provides the proper conditions for thoughts to grow. It matters not the thought, be it positive or negative, if concentrated upon sufficiently, it will flourish... —*Shantidasa*

When you have learned to control your mind in the face of disturbances, then your mind has acquired one pointedness... —*Patanjali*

The marvel of the living mind is that when it is illumined it can move into uncharted territories. It is enabled to take this step not out of reaction to the hurts of the past, but through the miracle of liberation from them...

—*Indira Gandhi*

The mind is like a fire which is fueled by thoughts and desires. If there are no thoughts or desires, then the fire of the mind will die out...

—*Lakshmana*

When the mind is stilled, when the intellect is stilled, that is called the highest state by the wise... —*The Upanishads*

Miracles

Miracles only happen to people who believe in them...

—*Anonymous*

Miracles only work through your own faith. Where there is no faith there can be no miracle. So he who wants to perform a miracle can only do so by the power of faith. From this it is evident that the matter rests entirely with you...

—*Papa Ramdas*

Moderation

If you have too much of anything, you cannot know yourself...

—*Bhagavan Das*

There should be balance in all our actions; to be either extreme or luke-warm is equally bad... —*Hazrat Inayat Khan*

Money

Whoever desires money never has enough of it, there always seems to be lack, and more never seems to be quite enough...

—*Anonymous*

Money can help you to get medicines, but not health. Money can help you to get soft pillows, but not sound sleep. Money can help you to get material comforts, but not eternal bliss. Money can help you get ornaments, but not beauty...

—*Sivananda*

Accumulated money brings misery to the owner. Keep money flowing... —*Papa Ramdas*

Nature

Nature is always trying to adjust itself and, in that adjustment, destruction also plays an important part...
—*Papa Ramdas*

What one has achieved can be attained by another. This is the grand law of Nature... —*Sivananda*

Every spring Nature writes a fresh, new chapter in the Book of Genesis... —*Anonymous*

Nature has devised a grand plan leading toward perfection. Life itself is one lengthy march to such an ideal using death as the process by which the tainted and the imperfect are recycled into another more enduring form... —*Shantidasa*

Leave all things to take their natural course, and do not interfere... —*Lao-tzu*

Nature never makes any fuss, and yet it does everything...
—*Lao-tzu*

Nothing/Emptiness

Your nothingness is the miraculous essence of God...
—*A Spiritual Warrior*

When you have reduced yourself to nothing—when your "self" has disappeared—when you have become nothing, then you are yourself God. The man who is nothing knows God, for God is nothing. Nothing is everything....
— *Yoga Swami*

There is nothing to do. Just be. Do nothing. Be. No climbing mountains and sitting in caves. I do not even say 'be yourself' since you do not know yourself. Just be...
—*Nisargadatta*

Become envious of anyone lower than you. You must become very small. In fact you must become nothing. Only a person who is nobody can abide in the Self...

—Ramana Maharshi

To be empty, completely empty, is not a fearsome thing; it is absolutely essential for the mind to be unoccupied; to be empty, unenforced, for then only it can move into unknown depths... *—J.Krishnamurti*

The game is not about becoming somebody, it's about becoming nobody... *—Ram Dass*

Out of emptiness arises compassion... *—Buddhist saying*

It is only because the sage does nothing that he can do everything... *—Lao-tzu*

Do not vainly lament but realize that nothing is permanent and learn from it the emptiness of life...*—Gautama Buddha*

When you demand nothing of the world, nor of God, when you want nothing, expect nothing, then the Supreme State will come to you uninvited and unexpected...*—Nisargadatta*

Nothing is brought into this world and nothing can be taken...

—Nityananda

Know that the world, although appearing as substantial, has nothing substantial in it: it is a void, being merely an appearance created by the images and vagaries of the mind...

—Yoga Vasistha

Power is emptiness and nothingness, as all definitions of yourself melt away, and you neither begin nor end...

—Maya Sarada Devi

Brahma is the Void, the Ancient Void of the spirit...

—The Upanishads

The Hebrew word "I" consists of the same letters as the word for "nothing."... —*Anonymous*

Sitting quietly, doing nothing, everything is achieved... —*Zen saying*

Emptiness is most powerful. It is all pervading. When the mind becomes still, you experience that emptiness within you.. Empty yourself and realize the truth...—*Papa Ramdas*

Old Age

Old as I am in age, I have no feeling that I have ceased to grow inwardly or that my growth will stop at the dissolution of my flesh... —*Mohandas Gandhi*

In your old age you will complete for the glory of God the tower of your soul that you began to build in the golden days of your youth... —*Mother Teresa*

Oneness

Seeing difference is ignorance. We are all one...—*Sankara*

There are no others... . —*Ramana Maharshi*

For him who sees him-Self in every self, in everything, there is no longer left any perplexity, doubt, sorrow, fear... —*The Upanishads*

All life is one. The world is one home. All are members of one human family. All creation is an organic whole. No man is independent of this whole. Man makes himself miserable by separating himself from others. Separation is death. Unity is eternal life... —*Sivananda*

God is an artist par excellence. He has painted the picturesque universe on the screen of His own immutable and glowing Spirit. So He is the painter and the painted... —*Papa Ramdas*

When the oneness of the totality of things is not recognized, then ignorance as well as particularization arises...

—*Ashvaghosa*

All humanity is one undivided and indivisible family...

—*Mohandas Gandhi*

The one is here, there and everywhere; there is not a pinhole where this one will not be found... —*Nityananda*

All life is one. Differences are superficial. They are only in the outer; they are only in the body. But one great common Consciousness dwells as the Reality within all names and forms, with all creatures, not only all human beings, in all creatures... —*Ramanujan*

When, to a man who understands, the Self has become all things, what sorrow, what trouble can there be to him who once beheld that oneness... —*The Upanishads*

When a person abstains from doing wrong to any creature, in thought, word, or deed, he is said to attain to the state of oneness with God... —*Mahabharata*

There is only one power that is active in every one of us and that is God...It is the one power that pervades the whole universe that is responsible for all activities and movements in the universe... —*Papa Ramdas*

You are the prison-house, you are the prisoner and you are the one who imprisons yourself... —*Vimala Thakar*

That which exists is one; sages call it by various names...

—*Vedic saying*

What the principle of oneness teaches us is that no matter how hard we try to act otherwise, we are all equals...

—*Anonymous*

In reality there are not two. There is only One...

—*Ramakrishna*

We go on believing we are separate. We are not—not even for a single moment. Drop the idea of separation–and the fear of death disappears. If you become one with the whole, you will live forever. You will go beyond birth and death...

—Rajneesh

I believe that if one man gains spiritually the whole world gains with him and, if one falls, the whole world falls to that extent... *—Mohandas Gandhi*

Look upon all and everything as images of One, namely God...

—Sathya Sai Baba

He who in his own soul perceives the Supreme Soul in all beings, and acquires equanimity towards all of them, attains the highest bliss... *—Manu*

Order

A secret force is at work trying to carry out a plan–a moral, spiritual plan to bring order out of the seeming chaos of creation... *—Paramahansa Yogananda*

Though we can't always see it at the time, if we look upon events with some perspective, we see things always happen for our best interests. We are being guided in a way better than we know ourselves... *—Satchidananda*

Pain

Pain is a blessing in disguise. Pain is an eye-opener. Pain is your silent teacher. Pain will turn your mind toward God...

—Sivananda

Pain is your teacher; pain is there for a reason...

—Satchidananda

When you cling to pain you only succeed in pouring more salt on the wound... *—Anonymous*

Miseries, though belonging to the world of dreams, are of a certainty painful, and do not vanish until we cease dreaming... —*Srimad Bhagavatam*

When the body is in pain, a distorted area of awareness is crying out to the rest of awareness for help...
—*Deepak Chopra*

Pain is the outcome of sin... —*Gautama Buddha*

When the mind is in tune with God, we shall be above the pains of the world... —*Papa Ramdas*

The world is so constructed that, if you wish to enjoy its pleasures, you must also endure its pains. Whether you like it or not, you cannot have one without the other...—*Brahmananda*

The cure for pain is in the pain... —*Rumi*

With proper understanding, the pain and the pleasure are the same. Both are lessons. In such a light, pain becomes pain no more. One who understands the world in the proper way will see the pain is there as a necessity, something to be risen above... —*Satchidananda*

Past

The past and the unknown do not meet at any point; they cannot be brought together by any act whatsoever; there is no bridge to cross over nor a path that leads to it...
—*J.Krishnamurti*

Of all sad words of tongue or pen the saddest are: "What might have been."... —*Anonymous*

Let us not raise the ghost of the past... —*Papa Ramdas*

That deed is not well done that one regrets when it is done...
—*Gautama Buddha*

Patience

In any contest between power and patience, bet on patience... —*Anonymous*

Slow down and the thing you are chasing will come around and catch you... —*Zen saying*

With time and patience the mulberry leaf becomes a silk gown... —*Oriental proverb*

A patient man cannot be irritated even a bit. Patience helps a man in the conquest of temper. Patience gives immense strength... —*Sivananda*

Be patient in your striving; be persistent in your expectations... —*Anonymous*

Patience gives you the power to practice; practice gives you the power that leads you to perfection... —*Yogi Bhajan*

Patience and silence go together... —*Paramananda*

True patience simply means having absolute confidence in God... —*Anonymous*

Patience is all the strength a man needs...—*Sathya Sai Baba*

Peace/Harmony

Peace is difficult to attain for those whose mind is centered on the body... —*Nityananda*

To the peaceful a house is like a forest and to the restless even a forest is like a crowded city. To one who is at peace, the entire world is a peaceful forest. To one who is restless with a thousand thoughts, it is an ocean of sorrow...
—*Yoga Vasistha*

Peace comes not from doing, but from undoing; not from getting, but from letting go... —*Satchidananda*

If you are inwardly free from fighting, no one will be able to start a fight with you... —*Anonymous*

Harmony means absence of conflict; it means stillness and silence, peace and tranquility... —*Ramesh Balsekar*

Undisturbed peace of mind is attained by the cultivation of friendliness toward the happy, compassion for the unhappy, delight in the virtuous, and indifference in the evil... —*Patanjali*

That man attains peace who, abandoning all desires, moves about without longing, without the sense of mine and without egoism... —*Bhagavad-Gita*

The thirst for objects is the greatest enemy of peace. Desire causes distraction of various sorts....The mind will be ever restless and hanker after the objects. When this thirst dies, man enjoys peace... —*Sivananda*

The world is not in need of saving, it is perfect in itself—it is not a mess to be fixed up. It is harmonious and whole, and it is our responsibility to harmonize with it, not change it... —*A Spiritual Warrior*

I was glad I was born, glad I suffered so, glad I did make big blunders, glad to enter peace... —*Vivekananda*

Each one has to find his peace from within. And peace to be real must be unaffected by outside circumstances... —*Mohandas Gandhi*

Peace of mind is worth any price it demands... —*Gayatri Devi*

Peace cannot suddenly descend from the heavens. It can only come when the root causes of trouble are removed... —*Jawaharlal Nehru*

Perfect peace can dwell only where all egotism has disappeared... —*Gautama Buddha*

Peace is the most priceless possession of man. It is the sign of a virtuous character... —*Sathya Sai Baba*

Peace is in that heart in which no wave of desire of any kind arises... This eternal peace is your real existence—it is not a state or truth to be attained but to be realized; because you are ever That... —*Papa Ramdas*

Everyone thirsts for peace, but few people understand that perfect peace cannot be obtained as long as the inner soul is not filled with the presence of God... —*Anandamayi Ma*

A peaceful mind is your most precious capital... —*Sivananda*

The first step to bringing peace into the world is to realize the peace that already dwells within you... —*Anonymous*

Perfection

There can never be a perfect world because the world is always a creation of an imperfect mind. A perfect object cannot be made by such an imperfect tool... —*Ramana Maharshi*

God is perfection itself, not an effort at perfection... —*Nisaragadatta*

The perfect man employs his mind as a mirror. It grasps nothing: It refuses nothing. It receives, but doesn't keep. Thus he can triumph over matter, without injury to himself... —*Lao-tzu*

Life is perfect exactly the way it is; no one ever said perfection must be consistent... —*Shantidasa*

Don't you see that it's all perfect?... —*Neem Karoli Baba*

When people reach the highest perfection, it is nothing special, it is their normal condition... —*Hindu saying*

Only in the deepest silence of the night the stars smile and whisper among themselves: vain is this (human) seeking: unbroken perfection is over all... —*Rabindranath Tagore*

They are the perfect men who, being such, out of the greatness of their loving hearts, make themselves small to slave continuously to make the imperfect ones perfect also...

—*Sufi saying*

In and with all your imperfections, YOU are perfect...

—*Sunyata*

People who seek perfection in their lives are setting themselves up for failure... —*Anonymous*

Perseverance

Perseverance is the ability to follow through on an idea long after the mood has passed... —*Anonymous*

The constant dripping of water wears away the stone...

—*Sufi saying*

Steady perseverance alone will tame your mind, and it is only through a tamed mind that you can experience God...

—*Sathya Sai Baba*

Take up one thing and do it, and see the end of it, and before you have seen the end, do not give up. Those who only take a nibble here and a nibble there will never attain anything... —*Vivekananda*

One cannot achieve anything lasting in this world by being irresolute... —*Mohandas Gandhi*

Pessimism

The optimist keeps his eye on the doughnut; the pessimist can only see the hole... —*Anonymous*

Pessimism likes to build walls where optimism builds bridges.... —*Anonymous*

Both the optimist and the pessimist are right, but as different as light is from darkness... —*Anonymous*

Possessions

If a man's happiness is due to outer causes and external possessions, then a man devoid of possessions should have no happiness whatever. Does real experience show this? No... —*Ramana Maharshi*

The moment you have a desire to possess something is the exact moment you enter into the first phase of enslavement to it... —*Anonymous*

The sense of possession is a great obstacle to the realization of God. Attachment to any external object narrows our vision, fosters egotism and gives rise to the false notion that we are separate from God... —*Papa Ramdas*

Whatever there be on the surface of the earth–property, gold, cattle, good health—none of these truly satisfy man. Tranquility arises from this understanding...—*Tibetan saying*

Of what can we be sure, except that whatever we have will soon be gone?... —*Yoga Vasistha*

You may possess things, but you must not be possessed by them... —*Aurobindo*

Possession of material riches, without inner peace, is like dying of thirst while bathing in a lake. If material poverty is to be avoided, spiritual poverty is to be abhorred. For it is spiritual poverty, not material lack, that lies at the core of all human suffering... —*Paramahansa Yogananda*

Self-mastery is a far greater possession than the possession of earth goods. If we do not possess ourselves, we may possess all the fine things of life and be unable to use them to any advantage... —*Paramanananda*

Material possessions are oftentimes a hindrance toward attaining higher consciousness. They take a cunning delight in becoming one's master while appearing as a benevolent slave... —*Shantidasa*

The emptiness of life cannot be satisfied by filling ourselves with possessions, although many people try... —*Anonymous*

What does not belong to you does not have the power to disturb you... —*Anonymous*

We try to acquire so many things of the world, but find no peace in them. When your mind is flitting from object to object....it lives in a state of restlessness which is itself misery. After possession of an object, comes care and anxieties; after a loss, grief and pain... —*Papa Ramdas*

Power

You gain power over another person in one of two ways: by winning his heart or by breaking his spirit... —*Anonymous*

Achievement gives power, but renunciation gives still more power... —*Hazrat Inayat Khan*

Desire for power acts like puffs of air which may blow out the lamp...that is being carefully tended... —*Sivananda*

All progress and infinite power is in every man's nature, only it is barred in and prevented from taking its proper course. If anyone can take the bar off, in rushes nature... —*Vivekananda*

You must yield up power over everyone... —*Patanjali*

No master cared a rap for occult powers for he has no need for them in his daily life... —*Ramana Maharshi*

Abusive power demonstrates itself by knocking down doors that are best unlocked with a key... —*Anonymous*

People want to demonstrate power, and that is a sickness even God cannot cure. It is beyond curing, and they call it "spiritual ego." When a man becomes a little spiritual and people start loving him and respecting him, giving him things, bowing to him, well, that's where the problem starts.... —*Yogi Bhajan*

Occult powers are heaps of rubbish... —*Ramakrishna*

Possession of powers causes intoxication of mind. He who possesses powers always misuses them. He wants to command, control and domineer over others. It is very difficult to renounce position and power... —*Sivananda*

Power entraps even when it is used to do good... —*Ram Dass*

Personal power lies in taking responsibility for yourself, not in assuming the responsibilities of other people... —*Anonymous*

A man is possessed of limited powers and is miserable; he wants to expand his powers so that he may be happy. But consider if it will be so; if with limited perceptions one is miserable, with extended perceptions the misery must increase proportionally... —*Ramana Maharshi*

He is the best of men who dislikes power... —*Mohammed*

True power is the falling away of individual identity... —*Maya Sarada Devi*

Prayer

Joy and thankfulness are the secret ingredients to all successful prayer... —*Anonymous*

The one who prays and the one to whom prayers are addressed are one and the same... —*Yoga Swami*

Prayer is a perpetual stillness of the heart, a surrendering to yourself as the aspect of God within you. Prayer is not beseeching an entity outside us for favours, but acknowledging the presence of God with us... —*A Spiritual Warrior*

Prayer is not an old woman's idle amusement. Properly understood and applied, it is the most potent instrument of action... —*Mohandas Gandhi*

Let us not pray to be sheltered from dangers but to be fearless in facing them. Let us not beg for the stilling of the pain but for the heart to conquer it... —*Rabindranath Tagore*

A heart-felt prayer is not recitation with the lips. It is a yearning from within which expresses itself in every word, every act, nay every thought of man... —*Mohandas Gandhi*

When you make prayer a moment of truth in your life, the heavens open in response... —*Anonymous*

The greatest prayer is patience... —*Gautama Buddha*

Prayer is not verbal. It is from the heart. To merge into the Heart is prayer... —*Ramana Maharshi*

The way you learn how to pray is to simply start praying... —*Shantidasa*

Prayer must be neutral if it is to be effective; once you lose your neutrality by asking for results, prayer becomes impotent... —*Anonymous*

Many people are praying for mountains to be moved when all they need to do is climb them... —*Anonymous*

Prayer needs no speech. It is in itself independent of any sensuous effort. But is must be combined with the utmost humility... —*Mohandas Gandhi*

If you ask of God, He gives you what you ask, but if you dare to live Him, God gives Himself and all that you would have asked for... —*Aurobindo*

Our prayers should be burning words coming forth from the furnace of a heart filled with love... —*Mother Teresa*

Pride

Humility does not strive; that's all pride knows how to do... —*Anonymous*

Too much learning makes one proud. One must bend one's head...realizing the limitations of reason. It can only take you to the gate and it has to be left behind when you enter the realm of the Spirit. You have to unlearn what you have learnt and become as simple and guileless as a child... —*Papa Ramdas*

God cannot be realized if there is the slightest trace of pride... —*Ramakrishna*

If you are discouraged, it is a sign of pride, because it shows you trust in your own powers... —*Mother Teresa*

Pride is a negative virtue; it exists to glorify humility... —*Sivananda*

Pride has no more value than a cock crowing on a dung heap... —*Anonymous*

Problems

Problems are messages... —*Shakti Gawain*

Stand back from the mountain of problems, refuse to acknowledge that they are yours, and they will dissolve and disappear before your eyes... —*Annamalai Swami*

Those who in this world have the courage to try and solve in their own lives new problems of life, are the ones who raise society to greatness... —*Rabindranath Tagore*

Each problem has hidden in it an opportunity so powerful that it literally dwarfs the problem. The great success stories were created by people who recognized a problem and turned it into an opportunity... —*Anonymous*

Every mistake is your best teacher. One has to evolve through sins and mistakes. They are inevitable... —*Sivananda*

A man cannot help going wrong and making mistakes as long as he is ignorant of his true nature... —*Paramananda*

The best way to solve a complex problem is to break it into pieces and solve it one piece at a time... —*Anonymous*

There is no problem unless you create one...—*Gayatri Devi*

We can magnify our problems and we can minimize them... —*Paramananda*

Do not be intimidated by problems. A problem is not a problem, only a challenge to be surmounted. Defiantly hoist your sails and sail into the prevailing wind. There are no storms sufficient to scuttle a ship when a positive attitude is taken... —*Shantidasa*

The solution to the problem of the day is the awakening of the consciousness of humanity to the divinity within... —*Hazrat Inayat Khan*

To be resentful of a problem only makes it heavier; to recognize and appreciate it always makes it lighter... —*Anonymous*

Misfortunes are great, but human beings are even greater than misfortune... —*Rabindranath Tagore*

You may ponder internally over your personal problems and try to seek guidance, but it may be only wasting your energy to think over the problems of others... —*Maharaj C. Singh*

All your problems arise because you have defined and therefore limited yourself. When you do not think yourself to be this or that, all conflict ceases... —*Nisargadatta*

Purpose

The only useful purpose of this birth is to turn within and realize. There is nothing else to do... —*Ramana Maharshi*

Where there is purpose there is ego. Play is no purpose. It gives joy. Play itself is the purpose. No object is to be gained by playing... —*Papa Ramdas*

The purpose of life is to unlearn what has been learned and to remember what has been forgotten... —*Sufi saying*

Man has come here with a definite purpose. Life is not meant merely for eating, drinking and procreating...
—*Sivananda*

You have a purpose only as long as you are not complete; until then, completeness, perfection, is the purpose. But when you are complete in yourself, fully integrated within and without, then you enjoy the universe; you do not labor at it... —*Nisargadatta*

Your sole business in life is to attain God-realization. All else is useless and worthless... —*Sivananda*

Relationship

The difficulty with relationships is that they blur boundaries that are used to determine who we really are...
—*Anonymous*

Relationship is a mirror into which your inner being gets reflected... —*Vimala Thakar*

Relationships fail because of unfulfilled expectations, and the greater the expectation, the more likely the failure...
—*Anonymous*

Our primary relationship is really with ourselves...Our relationships with other people constantly reflect exactly where we are in the process... —*Shakti Gawain*

In the face of the relationship with God, all other relations dwindle into nothing...the question of any domestic relationship...cannot arise... —*Papa Ramdas*

All of life is relationship... —*Swami Rama*

Your most important relationship is with yourself; most people form relationships to avoid themselves...
—*Anonymous*

Relationships fail because people try to change one another, thereby altering the chemistry that brought them together in the first place... —*Anonymous*

As travelers meet by chance on the way, so does man meet a wife, children, relatives, and friends; let him therefore be in the world and yet separate from it...—*Srimad Bhagavatam*

Religion

True religion must awaken in us a sense of joy...
—*Paramananda*

There is no such thing as God of one religion and God of another. We have made distinctions through our ignorance...
—*Papa Ramdas*

Every true faith began with something very good, but as they get old they become encrusted with dogma...
—*Peace Pligrim*

Religions and dogmas keep one looking for God...God is not external to us; no looking or searching is necessary—one need only abide within the consciousness of their realization of God's presence... —*A Spiritual Warrior*

Do you think that you can find God by worshipping another? You do such silly, stupid things—offering flowers and lighting candles! Do you think that you can find God by giving bribes?... —*Yoga Swami*

What cannot be followed out in day-to-day practice cannot be called religion... —*Mohandas Gandhi*

Where all religions meet is the realization in no mystical sense, but in the most worldly and everyday sense, that GOD IS EVERYTHING, AND EVERYTHING IS GOD...

—*Ramana Maharshi*

The religious man always thinks that his zeal for making converts is a virtue. It is not a virtue at all, but a vice, because this zeal is due to his egoism...

—*Lakshmana Sarma*

Religion is a bridge to the spiritual—but the spiritual lies beyond religion. Unfortunately, in seeking the spiritual we may become attached to the bridge rather than crossing over it... —*Prabhushri*

Too much religion kills God, the God in Man; enslaves him to superstition, instead of bringing him Freedom from all fear.... —*Bhagavan Das*

It is good to be born in a church, but it is bad to die there. It is good to be born a child, but bad to remain a child. Churches, ceremonies, symbols are good for children; but when the child is grown up, he must burst, either the church or himself...The end of all religion is the realization of God...

—*Vivekananda*

God is not imprisoned or caged within the four walls of temples or other religious places. He fills the universe and lives in devotees' hearts... —*Shirdi Sai Baba*

Doing good to others is the highest religion...

—*Anonymous*

A religion that is without joy is really no religion at all...

—*Anonymous*

If a religion does not teach love, respect, and regard for others, it cannot be the religion of humanity...—*Muktananda*

A sage once said: "It is good to be born into a church, but it is bad to die in a church," which meant that while we are born into a religion, we have no choice about it. As we grow up and expand in wisdom we should be tolerant and our love and sympathy and understanding should go beyond the borders of our own religion... —*Chidananda*

Religion, in one way or another, has always been with us. Religion will continue to always be with us. What needs to be discarded and thrown away is the ecclesiastical rubbish which binds us to religion instead of God... —*Shantidasa*

No religion has a monopoly on spirituality... —Anonymous

I maintain that Faith is a pathless land, and you can approach it by any path whatsoever, by any religion, by any sect...

—*J.Krishnamurti*

Never hurt the feelings of others. Speak the truth. Do not kill any sentient beings. Cultivate such divine virtues as humility, courage, forgiveness, tolerance and compassion. Love all, be kind to all. Be good, do good. Be charitable. Purify the heart. Serve humanity. Share what you have with others...Love thy neighbor as thyself...These, indeed, constitute the essentials of all religions... —*Sivananda*

Many religions claim that theirs is the only path to the Truth...But God never made an agreement with any of these religions. All religions are of fairly recent origin, but God has existed since the beginning of time. He could not have signed a contract with any religious founder saying, "You are my exclusive salesman."... —*Muktananda*

It is more important to create a safer, kinder world than to recruit more people to the religion that happens to satisfy us... —*Dalai Lama*

The religion of love is apart from all religions... —*Rumi*

God has no religion...

—*Mohandas Gandhi*

What counts is not creed but conduct...

—*Sarvepalli Radhakrishnan*

The religion of each is the attainment of his soul's desire. When he is on the path of that attainment he is religious. When he is off the path he is impious...—*Hazrat Inayat Khan*

God has no religion... —*Mohandas Gandhi*

So long as you have a creed, you have no God...—*Vivekananda*

All the disharmony of the world caused by religious differences is the result of man's failure to understand that religion is one, truth is one, God is one: how can there be two religions... —*Anonymous*

Different creeds are but different paths to reach the Almighty... —*Ramakrishna*

Like the bee gathering honey from different flowers, the wise man accepts the essence of different Scriptures and sees only the good in all religions... —*Srimad Bhagavatam*

Religion is not what is grasped by the brain, but a heart grasp...
—*Mohandas Gandhi*

Common men talk bagfuls of religion but act not a grain of it, while the wise man speaks little, but his whole life is a religion acted out... —*Ramakrishna*

Religion is something which every individual must work out for himself; and we cannot call ourselves religious until through our life we prove the reality of God and the reality of our own soul... —*Paramananda*

Religions were never designed to unite man. They were supposed to unite man and God. They failed in both because they never realized that in the unity of human being, God is born... —*Babu Rao Patel*

One can become so attached to the outward symbols and structure of religion that one forgets its original intent—to bring one closer to God...

—*Peach Pilgrim*

Saints

A person remains ordinary as long as he is led by the mind: but freed from the mind, he becomes a great saint...

—*Nityananda*

The beginning of saintliness is killing of egoism. The end of saintliness is Eternal Life. The key to saintliness is chastity. The light of saintliness is universal love... —*Sivananda*

There are no external signs to mark out a God-realized saint. He does not grow a horn. But he is always full of bliss. He is happy under all conditions... —*Papa Ramdas*

A man may have never entered a church or a mosque, nor performed any ceremony; but if he realizes God within himself, and is thereby lifted above the vanities of the world, that man is a holy man, a saint, call him what you will...

—*Vivekananda*

The true saint goes in and out amongst the people and eats and sleeps with them and buys and sells in the market and marries and takes part in social intercourse and never forgets God for a single moment...

—Abu Sa'id Ibn

Every Saint has the same message to give and the same teachings to impart. No Saint, no perfect Master, comes into this world to create a religion, to divide people, to set one nation against another or one religion against another. They come only to show us the Way which leads back to our original Home ...

—Charan Singh

Even saints who engage in no outward work bestow, through their thoughts and holy vibrations, more precious benefits on the world than can be given by the most strenuous humanitarian activities of unenlightened men...

—Paramahansa Yogananda

A Saint is like a tree. He does not call anyone, neither does he send anyone away. He gives shelter to whoever cares to come... *—Anandamayee Ma*

Saints are like big steamships which not only cross the ocean themselves but carry many passengers to the other shore...

—Ramakrishna

Why were saints, saints? Because they were cheerful when it was difficult to be cheerful, patient when it was difficult to be patient, and because they pushed on when they wanted to stand still, and kept silent when they wanted to talk; and were agreeable when they wanted to be disagreeable. That was all. It was quite simple and always will be...*—Anonymous*

One cannot expect to become a saint without paying the price, and the price is much renunciation, much temptation, much struggle and persecution, and all sorts of sacrifice... *—Mother Teresa*

Every prophet and every saint hath a way, but it leads to God: all the ways are really one... —*Rumi*

The first characteristic of a Saint is that he is calm and tranquil, and bears like a diamond the buffets of misfortune... —*Tukaram*

Great sages and saints have set certain rules for us to follow. If we followed those rules we shall know what is right and what is wrong so that we may avoid certain things... —*Papa Ramdas*

Search/Look Within

There is no search or goal possible, we are spiritually free and united in oneness with the absolute...The search is the ego's looking for itself, an illusory game of hide and seek... —*A Spiritual Warrior*

Be a lamp unto your own feet; do not seek outside yourself... —*Gautama Buddha*

The search for God is always futile because God can never be found, ever, simply because God has never been lost... —*Anonymous*

When ye leave off seeking you will experience that there was never anything to seek for. You were only seeking to lose something, when you went forth so vigorously in search... —*Sunyata*

There is only one temple, and that is the temple of yourself. And to find God you have to know this temple of yourself. There is no other temple. No one can save you... —*Yoga Swami*

We have all to return to the source. Every human being is seeking its source and must one day come to it. We must come from the within; we have gone outward; now we must return inward... —*Ramana Maharshi*

Remember, you cannot abandon what you do not know. To go beyond yourself you must know yourself...—*Nisargadatta*

Look within. Within you is the hidden God. Within you is the immortal Soul. Within you is the inexhaustible spiritual treasure. Within you is the ocean of bliss. Look within for the happiness which you have sought in vain...

—*Sivananda*

Riches and power may vanish because they are outside ourselves. Only that which is within can we call our own...

—*Hazrat Inayat Khan*

At the end of all religious paths there is the quest 'Who am I ?' Until that question is satisfactorily answered no one can claim to know what the truth is or what God is. The ultimate instruction in all religions should therefore be 'Know thyself'... —*Lakshmana*

He who knows others is wise. He who knows himself is enlightened... —*Lao-tzu*

You have everything. You are the whole world. Why? Because the kingdom of God is within you. Then why do you want to run about and beg?... —*Yoga Swami*

As we go deeper within ourselves we are less inclined to notice outer happenings... —*Parmananda*

Look within. Seek the Self. There will be an end of the world and its miseries...The enquiry "Who am I?" is the only method of putting an end to all misery and ushering in supreme Beatitude... —*Ramana Maharshi*

Most people are standing on a mountain of gold looking at a pile of silver in the distance... —*Anonymous*

The world is ready to give up its secrets if we only know how to knock, how to give it the necessary blow...—*Vivekananda*

What you are trying to find out is what you already are...
—*Nisargadatta*

The path to the source of your and the world's being is not without. You have to go within yourself. 'Seek within and know thyself' these secret and sublime hints come to us wafted from the breath of Rishis (wise men) through the dust of ages...
—*Papa Ramdas*

People try to find out about things which are outside of them before they try to find out "Who am I?"...—*Ramana Maharshi*

Every man is engaged in searching for something lost. Life is the chance afforded him to recover the peace and the joy he has lost...
—*Sathya Sai Baba*

If you search in deep water only, you will find the pearl. If you keep to the shore, you will find broken shells only...
—*Sivananda*

Many millions search for God and find Him in their hearts...
—*Sikh proverb*

In the search for truth there are certain questions that are not important. Of what material is the universe constructed? Is the universe eternal? Are there limits or not to the universe? What is the ideal form of organization for human society? If a man were to postpone his search and practice for Enlightenment until such questions were solved, he would die before he found the path...
—*Gautama Buddha*

Man is the reflection of God; but the reflection cannot exist without the object reflected; so man must know what God is, if he would know himself. This has been the search down the ages and this search must be made by every individual for himself; there is no one who can answer this question for another...
—*Paramananda*

Oh friend, where are you going? Where have you come from, and what are you supposed to do? You belong to the supreme Truth, but you have forgotten your origin. Now is the time to get back on the main road... —*Muktananda*

All search is vain, until we begin to perceive that wisdom is within ourselves...then we may know the sun is rising, that the morning is breaking for us... —*Vivekananda*

In truth, we seek God outside of ourselves until we make the great Discovery—which is that our heart is the sanctuary where the Lord of the universe dwells in all His glory...

—*Papa Ramdas*

We go here, there, to this place, to that one, always looking for the happiness that is there inside... —*Satchidananda*

Why does a man go out to look for God? It is your own heart beating, and you do not know, you were mistaking it for something outside... —*Vivekananda*

Where do you go in search of God? He is with you... —*Kabir*

Self-Esteem

Self-esteem stems from positive beliefs about yourself; it does not depend upon the approval of another person...

—*Anonymous*

Esteem by others or self-esteem, which is better?...The more you depend on others for esteem, the less you are self-sufficient... —*Lao-tzu*

Don't let the opinions of other people determine the image you have of yourself. There is no need to feel either appreciated or understood. Be even-minded. What you think about yourself is everything. What others think about you has no value at all, unless you choose to give it value...

—*Shantidasa*

Do not imagine that any one can have true faith in God who has not faith in himself... —*Paramananda*

You must see God inside of you before you recognize it in another human being... —*Ma Jaya Sati Bhagavati*

Putting someone else high upon a pedestal is just another way of putting yourself down... —*Anonymous*

Selfishness

If you always seek your own advantage, what is the use of remaining among men? A selfish man frustrates every chance to make all beings rejoice... —*Tibetan saying*

Every act of selfishness or thought of selfishness makes us attached to something, and immediately we are made slaves... —*Vivekananda*

A selfish man is always miserable. He has neither peace nor happiness... —*Sivananda*

Any idea that is built on selfishness will disturb your mind... —*Satchidananda*

Selfishness keeps man blind through life...Life is a misery for the man who is absorbed in himself...—*Hazrat Inayat Khan*

Selfishness is a negative virtue; it exists to glorify selflessness... —*Sivananda*

Master pride and dame vanity have mingled and given birth to an ogre named "selfishness"... —*Shantidasa*

Greed is the chief officer of passion. Wherever there is greed, there is passion; and where there is passion, there is greed almost invariably. The understanding gets clouded, the intellect gets perverted, and the memory gets confused by passion and greed... —*Sivananda*

The selfish man can stand up to his chin in water and still be thirsty... —*Anonymous*

Self-Realization

Self-realization is nothing but seeing God literally. Our greatest mistake is that we think of God as acting symbolically and allegorically, instead of practically and literally...You must get rid of the idea that you are yet to realize the Self. You are the Self here and now... —*Ramana Maharshi*

The awareness of being the witness of everything is the secret of self-realization... —*Sathya Sai Baba*

Realizations are personal, one cannot borrow or have the same realization as another person, nor can one take the same path...With realization, spirit abides in itself. Communion is within the whole, freedom is its essence. The absolute is, and I never was separate... —*A Spiritual Warrior*

Self-realization means I am completely full, I don't want to know anything, I don't require anything at all now...
—*Nisargadatta*

One cannot get a true feeling about God from the study of books...books, scriptures and science appear as mere dirt and straw after the realization of God... —*Ramakrishna*

Human life has been given to you for the sole purpose of realizing the Self. If you die without realizing the Self your life has been wasted. Death can come at any time...
—*Annamalai Swami*

Man's ultimate aim is the realization of God, and all of his activities—social, religious—have to be guided by the ultimate aim of the vision of God... —*Mohandas Gandhi*

At the point of realization there is no ego. That's when the shadow realizes it's a shadow... —*Satchidananda*

Self-realization is real religion, all the rest is only preparation—hearing lectures, or reading books, or reasoning, is merely preparing the ground; it is not religion...

—Vivekananda

The Self is hidden in the deepest cave of the heart...

—The Upanishads

The realized man finds himself in others — they are not different from himself. With wise men he is wise, but with ignorant men he becomes ignorant, with children he will play and with the learned he will be scholarly...

—Ramana Maharshi

Self-realization means that we have been consciously connected with our Source of being. Once we have made this connection then nothing can go wrong... *—Paramananda*

No one is ever away from his Self and therefore everyone is in fact Self-realized; only—and this is a great mystery—people do not know this and want to realize the Self. Realization consists only in getting rid of the false idea that one is not realized. It is not anything new to be acquired...

—Ramana Maharshi

Who stands already on heaven's topmost dome needs not to search for ladders... *—Rumi*

For realization, effort is needed but grace is also required, and grace is more important... *—Lakshmana*

Self-Reliance

Don't believe anyone who promises to help you. No one will help you because no one can. Another may point the way, but you have to do the walking... *—Yoga Swami*

You are your own physician. You are your own savior and redeemer. Nobody can give you freedom. You will have to tread the spiritual path yourself. Rely on your own self-exertion. Teachers and books can only help you to a certain extent... *Sivananda*

Self-reliance as commonly understood is ego–reliance and it worsens bondage. Reliance on God alone is true self-reliance... *—Ramana Maharshi*

Remember this point well. No one can save another. You will have to depend upon yourself alone... *—Sivananda*

You must rely upon yourself. The influence of a saint may give you a push on the spiritual path, but you have to tread the path yourself... *—Ramcharandas*

If another drinks, does it quench your thirst? If another eats, does it appease your hunger? If another sleeps, does it rest you? Who, then, shall develop your understanding?... *—Gautama Buddha*

Mankind has a way of proclaiming self-reliance in a loud voice, but seldom is the dependency upon a higher force for every breath ever mentioned... *—Anonymous*

There is no virtue greater than self-reliance. The possession of this important quality is a *sine qua non* for all aspirants who search after Truth... *—Sivananda*

Self-help is the capacity to stand on one's legs without anybody's help... *—Mohandas Gandhi*

God gives food to every bird, but he does not throw it into the nest... *—Hindu saying*

To blame society for one's own deficiency is like blaming the pillow for the headache one suffers...*—Sathya Sai Baba*

True self-reliance does not mean reliance on one's physical strength; it means reliance on something mightier, something which is less perishable...It means trusting in the spiritual... *—Paramananda*

Service

Service is the rent we pay for our place on earth...
—*Anonymous*

To bring joy to one heart with love—is better than a thousand litanies...
—*Sufi saying*

He is the greatest man who is the servant of all...—*Sivananda*

If you make your mind pure, you automatically help everyone in the world because each person will receive a cleansing and healing measure of your own purity... —*Annamalai Swami*

Trying to help the world without knowing yourself will be just like a blind man trying to treat the diseases of the eyes of others. First, clear your own eyes... —*Ramana Maharshi*

Life is best spent in alleviating pain, assuaging distress, and promoting peace and joy. The service of man is more valuable than what you call "service to God." God has no need of your service. Please man, you please God...—*Sathya Sai Baba*

The highest service is, after getting for yourself the knowledge of the Divine, to share with others that knowledge and rouse in their hearts devotion for and faith in God...
—*Papa Ramdas*

At the heart of silence is prayer. At the heart of prayer is faith. At the heart of faith is life. At the heart of life is service...
—*Mother Teresa*

Good works are valuable only as a means of becoming free. They do good to the doer, never to any other...—*Vivekananda*

He who has seen, known and realized most fully the truth of the identity of all selves in the one Self, he is the greatest and most free and willing servant... —*Bhagavan Das*

All other pleasures and possessions pale into nothingness before service which is rendered in a spirit of joy...

—*Mohandas Gandhi*

No one has ever risen to the real stature of spiritual maturity until they have found it finer to serve someone else than to serve themselves... —*Anonymous*

The best way for one to serve the world is to win the egoless state. If you are anxious to help the world but think you cannot do so by attaining the egoless state, then surrender to God all the world's problems along with your own...

—*Ramana Maharshi*

Love lies in service. Only that which is done not for fame or name, nor for appreciation or thanks of those for whom it is done, is life's service... —*Hazrat Inayat Khan*

Service is like a burning candle: it lights the path for others while consuming itself... —*Anonymous*

He only does not live in vain who employs his wealth, his thought, his speech to advance the good of others...

—*Hindu proverb*

If your loyalty is to your family, you are a servant of the family; if it is to God, you are a servant of God...

—*Sathya Sai Baba*

I am the servant of servants... —*Krishna*

I slept and dreamt that life was joy. I awoke and saw that life was service. I acted and behold, service was joy...

—*Rabindranath Tagore*

I can't help thousands. I can help only the one who stands before me... —*Mother Teresa*

Always try to serve others. Don't even call it helping, call it service because you are benefitted by that. If a man begs from you and you give him something, you shouldn't think you are helping him. Instead, he is helping you...

—*Satchidananda*

The purpose of life is to increase the warm heart. Think of other people. Serve other people sincerely. No cheating...

—*Dalai Lama*

Down in their hearts, the wise men know this truth: the only way to help yourself is to help others... —*Anonymous*

Service without humility is selfishness and egotism...

—*Mohandas Gandhi*

Silence

There is silence when you realize that there is nothing to gain and nothing to lose... —*Yoga Swami*

Silence gives us a new way of looking at something...

—*Mother Teresa*

As long as someone cries out "Oh God! Oh God!" be sure that he has not found God, for whoever has found him becomes still... —*Ramakrishna*

Silence has a wonderful creative power. Make a study of the lives of great men. They conceive an idea but they do not go out and shout it to the world; they think silently and work quietly until they realize their ideal... —*Paramananda*

A periodical decree of silence is not a torture but a blessing... —*Mohandas Gandhi*

We need to find God, but we cannot find Him in noise, in excitement. See how nature, the trees, the flowers, the grass grow in deep silence. See how the stars, the moon, and the sun move in silence... —*Mother Teresa*

Verily, he who speaks noble truths, and gives utterance to the Word of God, observes the vow of silence. Silence is restraint of speech... —*Srimad Bhagavatam*

Silence is the language of the Real... —*Sunyata*

The only language able to express the wholeness of truth is silence. Silence is our eternal speech. Silence is ever speaking. It is a perennial flow of language which is interrupted by speaking... —*Ramana Maharshi*

Silence of the sewn-up lips is no silence. One may achieve the same result by chopping off one's tongue, but that too would not be silence. He is silent who, having the capacity to speak, utters no idle word... —*Mohandas Gandhi*

Silence is the language of God: it is also the language of the heart... —*Sivananda*

The most important thing is silence....We cannot place ourselves directly in God's presence without imposing upon ourselves interior and exterior silence... —*Mother Teresa*

Simplicity

Our purpose in life is to realize the Self. It is an easy matter to get a little food and find somewhere congenial to live and meditate. Once we have achieved this we should have no further interest in the world and its problems...

—*Annamalai Swami*

People don't want simplicity, they want something complicated... —*Lakshmana*

A man who has gained access to Divinity, he has simplified his whole life... —*Paramananda*

Simple living will help you to control thoughts. If you lead a simple life, you have only very few wants and you will have to think a little only... —*Sivananda*

Simplicity of life is the true secret of happiness. Unhampered experience of joy which lies within comes out of simplicity. Your life should never be complicated with too many things... —*Chidananda*

Simplicity is the nature of great souls. They live and serve as incense burners... —*Papa Ramdas*

Smile

The knowers of truth...are happy and smiling all the time... —*Yoga Vasistha*

We shall never know all the good that a simple smile can do... —*Mother Teresa*

There are two kinds of smiles, genuine and artificial. Very often we put on smiles, but the heart does not smile, only the lips and face take part in it. This is not a real smile. When the heart is filled with joy, it is reflected on the face as a smile. It is a natural outflow of joy... —*Papa Ramdas*

If you can smile here and now with only that which is presently available, then life is lived to the fullest...—*Narayana*

Let no one ever come to you without leaving better and happier...to children, to the poor, to all who suffer and are lonely, give always a happy smile... —*Mother Teresa*

Solitude

The best of all is to Be alone to experience one's soul in Silence. To be nakedly alone, unseen, is better than anything in the world, a relief like death. To Be–alone–is one of life's greatest delights... —*Sunyata*

A man attached to desire cannot get solitude, wherever he may be; a detached man is always in solitude...

—*Ramdas Maharshi*

You will easily get illumination in solitude. Solitude has its charms. Prepare yourself for life in seclusion...—*Sivananda*

No time is ever wasted that is spent in wordless solitude...
—*Anonymous*

A religious man is a man who is Alone—not lonely, you understand, but Alone–with no theories or dogmas, no opinion, no background; he is alone and enjoying it...
—*J. Krishnamurti*

Should you band together the legs of two birds with a short rope an interesting phenomenon will take place. Each bird will hamper the other during their attempts to fly. Both birds will remain grounded. The same analogy can be applied to spiritual matters. Self-realization is a solitary affair in which each pilgrim must travel unhindered, alone...
—*Shantidasa*

Solitude is not to be found in forests only. It can be had even in towns and the thick of worldly occupation...
—*Ramana Maharshi*

Eagles fly alone; sheep herd together... —*Sufi saying*

Speech

In speech, we can only speak fragments of the truth, thus all speech misses the point; at best it is the partial expression of the inner feeling, but it can never grasp the totality of our heart–thus speech mostly divides, and rarely unites...
—*A Spiritual Warrior*

If you propose to speak, always ask yourself–Is it true, is it necessary, is it kind?... —*Gautama Buddha*

Those who speak with discretion are respected by mankind, as the sun, emerging from the shadows, by its rays creates great warmth... —*Tibetan saying*

The instant you speak about a thing, you miss the mark...
—*Zen saying*

One should speak what is true; one should speak what is sweet; one should not speak what is true if it is not sweet or what is sweet if it is false; this is the ancient law... —*Manu*

An enormous amount of energy is wasted by excessive talking. The energy that is spent talking should be carefully and vigilantly conserved and utilized for spiritual practices and in divine contemplation. The organ of speech distracts the mind considerably. A talkative man cannot dream of having peace even for a short time... —*Sivananda*

Speak to everyone in accordance with his level of understanding...—*Sufi saying*

Speak soft and sweet; sympathize with suffering and loss and ignorance; try your best to apply the salve of smoothing words and timely succor... —*Sathya Sai Baba*

We are ruined by foolish speech and saved by silence...
—*Hindu saying*

He who knows Tao does not care to speak of it; and he who is ever willing to speak of it does not know it... —*Lao-tzu*

We say little when we talk about ourselves... —*Anonymous*

Spirituality

In the spiritual life, all paths lead to the same place...
—*Satchidananda*

Our spiritual being is here to experience the process of life, not hold it stagnant, or try to control and possess it.... Our spirit cannot be free if it is desirous of controlling life, or if it is attached to the results of its actions...—*A Spiritual Warrior*

Are we not all divine? Are we not all made for a higher life?...
—*Mother Teresa*

In order to make spiritual progress you must be patient like a tree and humble like a blade of grass... —*Lakshmana*

Life in the world and life in the spirit are not incompatible... —*The Upanishads*

The universe is a more spiritual entity than we thought. The real fact is that we are in the midst of a spiritual world which dominates the material... —*Bhagavan Das*

Whatever draws the mind outward is unspiritual and whatever draws the mind inward is spiritual...—*Ramana Maharshi*

The spiritual life does not demand that we give up everything. We give up nothing, but we fill everything with the richness of feeling... —*Paramananda*

Our spiritual life is a life of dependence on God... —*Mother Teresa*

We are born into a world of nature; our second birth is into a world of spirit... —*Bhagavad-Gita*

Spirituality is the process of getting our minds off ourselves and back of God... —*Anonymous*

The first sign of spirituality is cheerfulness... —*Anonymous*

The grand secret of humanity is its inability to perceive its own spiritual character. Mankind is nothing less than miniature gods in the unfolding. When the ancient masters bid their students "To know thyself," they were merely guiding them to this sacred knowledge... —*Shantidasa*

Just as a candle cannot burn without fire, men cannot live without a spiritual life... —*Gautama Buddha*

You are going to develop a new kind of love, not physical but spiritual. That is not true love. Physical love is attachment. Spiritual love is born of oneness with the spirit...Therefore, rise up and declare that you are the immortal Spirit... —*Papa Ramdas*

Fearlessness is the first requisite of the spiritual life... *—Mohandas Gandhi*

Spiritual life cannot force out of anyone more than the person wishes to put into it... *—Gayatri Devi*

Success

Every worthwhile accomplishment, big or little, has its stages of drudgery and triumph; a beginning, a struggle, and a victory... *—Anonymous*

God doesn't require us to succeed, he only requires that you try... *—Mother Teresa*

Success is... a series of glorious defeats...*—Mohandas Gandhi*

Your greatest triumphs are not in winning, but in rising again after every fall... *—Anonymous*

Success in life has been achieved when all that one wants is finely balanced by all that one needs... *—Sufi saying*

Put your heart, mind, intellect and soul even into your smallest acts. This is the secret of success... *—Sivananda*

Progress in the spiritual path as well as success in the world, is impossible if you do not cultivate this cardinal virtue of keeping your word... *—Sivananda*

What people call an overnight success is generally the result of years of intensive preparation... *—Anonymous*

Suffering

Sorrow makes a man think of God.... Every man from king to peasant has a certain amount of sorrow. Even in cases where it seems absent, it is only a time factor that makes you think so–sooner or later it comes...One man may not question sorrow or God at the first blow but he is likely to do so at

the fifth blow. We have taken this vehicle in order to know our real state...
—*Ramana Maharshi*

All...suffering can be avoided by realizing that God is the only reality. You are the manifestation of God, a spiritual being emanating from the one and only source, which is God. Your spirit is eternal–you live, breathe and have your being in God. You cannot be separated from God, for God is the totality and the only reality–God "is," nothing else is...
—*A Spiritual Warrior*

You suffer from yourself alone; no one compels you...
—*Gautama Buddha*

If you come to see with clarity that the world is only a projection of the mind, you will transcend all suffering...
—*Subramania Bharati*

Suffering gives us the impetus to escape from our self-limiting ignorance. If God did not send these gifts of suffering and misery, many people would be content to live their whole lives alienated from God and ignorant of their true nature...
—*Annamalai Swami*

We humans, not God, create pain and suffering...
—*Mother Teresa*

God is in all humans, but all humans are not in God; that is the reason they suffer...
—*Ramakrishna*

Suffering turns the mind towards God. Suffering infuses mercy in the heart and softens it. Suffering strengthens. Suffering produces dispassion....Therefore, suffering is a blessing in disguise. It is the best thing in this world...
—*Sivananda*

When someone beats a rug with a stick, he is not beating the rug–his aim is to get rid of the dust from the veil of I-ness and that dust will not leave all at once. With every cruelty and every blow, it departs little by little, from the heart's face, sometimes in sleep and sometimes in wakefulness...

—*Rumi*

If you see suffering all around you, it is just a reflection of your own inner suffering. If you want to alleviate suffering, go to the root cause which is the suffering inside yourself...

—*Rumi*

Suffering is caused by desire; desire can be eradicated...

—*Gautama Buddha*

You add just as much suffering to the world when you take offense as when you give offense... —*Anonymous*

Spiritual suffering is a contradiction in term–symbols; spirit does not suffer; suffering is not spiritual... —*Sunyata*

The soul that is without suffering does not feel the need of knowing the ultimate cause of the universe. Sickness, grief and hardships are all indispensable elements in the spiritual ascent... —*Anandamayi Ma*

The more you move towards the goal, all sorrow will cease. Even if there is sorrow, you will become impervious to it. It will not touch you. There will be an inner strength created within you where even sorrow will not have a meaning for you. You will smile even at misfortune and suffering...

—*Chidananda*

People wail aloud that they are suffering and they are destitute, but very few turn away from the sources of their suffering and destitution... —*Yoga Vasistha*

In spite of warnings, admonitions, advice, and appeals that he should not submerge himself in the trivial and the transitory, man is still drawn towards misery by defects in his understanding... —*Sathya Sai Baba*

The cause of all our sufferings is in ourselves alone, not outside...Suffering turns men toward their Creator...
—Ramana Maharshi

You are not here to cry about the miseries of the human condition, but to change them when you find them not to your liking through joy, strength and vitality that is within you... *—Seth*

We are like thirsty souls running away from a spring of fresh water. We run away from that which would bring us what we are seeking. No wonder we have miseries...Miseries come because we do not listen to the voice within...*—Paramananda*

Do not close your eyes before suffering. Find ways to be with those who are suffering by all means, including personal contact and visits...By such means, awaken yourself and others to the reality of suffering in the world... *—Gautama Buddha*

If you train yourself to rejoice in suffering, if you think that everything is done by God for one's own betterment and uplift, if you welcome pain as a messenger of God to make you remember Him...then pain will not be pain any more. Suffering will not be suffering anymore... *—Sivananda*

All worldly pursuits have but one unavoidable and inevitable end, which is sorrow: acquisitions end in dispersion; buildings, in destruction; meetings, in separation; births, in death... *—Milarepa*

As long as you identify yourself with the body-mind, you are vulnerable to sorrow and suffering... *—Nisargadatta*

Suffering is a device to turn one's thoughts in the direction of God... *—Sufi saying*

Suffering bravely borne brings inner enfoldment...
—Paramananda

All troubles and suffering contain the hidden seeds of good... To shake the mind into wakefulness, God at times sends pain and disease. They serve to open up the eyes to the unrealities of this earthly life... —*Sivananda*

Suffering is due entirely to clinging or resisting; it is a sign of unwillingness to move on, to flow with life...—*Nisargadatta*

Surrender

If one surrenders completely, there will be no one left to ask questions...Surrender can never be regarded as complete as long as the devotee wants this or that from God... —*Ramana Maharshi*

Really, you don't lose anything by renouncing. Instead you become owner of the entire world. A homeless man can claim every home as his own. A pocket less man can thrust his hand into every pocket... —*Satchidananda*

When water surrenders to the flow of the river it reaches the ocean, so also must we surrender in order to reach our Source... —*Anonymous*

He that will not surrender himself to God's grace has to suffer worries without end, while the devotee that cultivates the attitude of surrender is free from cares, and therefore happy, even now... —*Lakshmana Sarma*

Spiritual maturity lies in the readiness to let go of everything. The giving up is the first step. But the real giving up is in realizing that there is nothing to give up, for nothing is your own... —*Nisargadatta*

God can only help you if you surrender to God... —*Saradamma*

Giving up something in the hope of getting something else in its place is not really giving up... —*U.G. Krishnamurti*

Surrender and all will be well. Throw all responsibility on God. Do not bear the burden...If one surrenders to God, there will be no cause for anxiety. Nothing will affect you...God never forsakes one who has surrendered...

—Ramana Maharshi

When surrender is complete, everything is God. Everything that happens is then His action. In that state there is peace, harmony and an absence of thoughts...*—Annamalai Swami*

Surrendering yourself to God is giving up what you can't keep in order to realize what you can't lose... *—Shantidasa*

A completely renounced person has no want at all. And the minute he stops wanting anything, he has his Self...

—Satchidananda

The Master gives himself up to whatever the moment brings...

—Lao-tzu

In order to let go of something, first you must know what it is... *—Nisargadatta*

When you surrender to God and agree to be guided from within, life becomes an adventure into the unknown...

—Anonymous

Energy arises from surrender to God. Energy comes from the heart expanding. A small, closed heart has no energy...

—Sathya Sai Baba

The true meaning of...surrender is the complete wearing away of the ego-sense, which is individuality...

—Lakshmana Sarma

We must empty ourselves to be filled with God. Even God cannot fill what is full... *—Mother Teresa*

Surrender is giving oneself up to the original cause of one's being. Do not delude yourself by imaging this source to be some God outside oneself. One's source is within oneself. Give yourself up to it... —*Ramana Maharshi*

Self-surrender is the surrender of all concern. It cannot be done, but it happens spontaneously when you realize your true nature. Verbal self-surrender, even accompanied by feeling, is of little value and breaks down under stress... —*Nisargadatta*

The only real surrender is that in which the poise is undisturbed by any adverse circumstance, and the individual, amidst every kind of hardship, is resigned with perfect calm to the will of God... —*Meher Baba*

If you want to be given everything, give up everything... —*Lao-tzu*

There is no loss in total, unreserved self-surrender. It is not at all a bad bargain. It is a mighty gain indeed...—*Sivananda*

Surrender can take effect only when it is done with full knowledge as to what real surrender means...—*Ramana Maharshi*

Surrender does not mean inaction. Surrender is action done on the Divine plane... —*Papa Ramdas*

Teacher

Divine knowledge is realized, not taught...—*Shirdi Sai Baba*

Teachers are of two breeds, those who teach us how to be, and those who teach us how not to be... —*Anonymous*

Your own self is your ultimate teacher. The outer teacher is merely a milestone. It is your inner teacher that will walk with you to the goal, for he is the goal... —*Nisargadatta*

The wise man is always a student. He is ever eager to learn. He never poses to be a teacher...A man of little learning

and little understanding is ever eager to teach. He wants to take up the role of preceptor. He is not eager to learn...
—Sivananda

The teacher, however great, can never give his knowledge to the pupils...although...he can kindle the light if the oil is in the lamp... *—Hazrat Inayat Khan*

We are all teachers of one another during our earthly pilgrimage, some greater teachers than others, but nevertheless, all teachers... *—Anonymous*

The best teacher is always heart to heart silence...
—Ramana Maharshi

A person seeking to escape from prison would be wise to seek the advice of someone who has escaped from that prison; a person seeking God would be wise to seek someone who has found God... *—Shantidasa*

I give people what they want, so eventually they'll want what I have to give... *—Shirdi Sai Baba*

Gurus and teachers only show the spiritual path, remove doubts and give some inspiration. You are the redeemer...You have to tread the spiritual path yourself...
—Sivananda

A teacher is one who communicates out of personal experience to someone who is interested in learning...
—Vimala Thakur

It is said that someone who acts as an enemy toward you is your best teacher... *—Dalai Lama*

Teachers can only bring the food; we must eat it to be nourished... *—Vivekananda*

When the pupil is ready, the teacher will appear...
—Zen saying

The Guru (teacher) is the person who discovers that you have fallen into a wrong road that leads into further and further darkness. For he knows the right road and he is full of love for all who strive to escape the travails of the night, without lamps to light their steps... —*Sathya Sai Baba*

Be with the world, but be not of it. Worldly duties are not ties. The world is the best teacher... —*Sivananda*

The first teacher is the mother; then the next teacher is the father; then the environment; and then God...—*Yogi Bhajan*

Any attempt to share an experience would be a very weak dilution of the original experience. A peasant cannot begin to understand the royal life just because he has changed to catch a momentary glimpse of a king... —*Anonymous*

Learning is not the accumulation of knowledge. Learning is movement from moment to moment... —*J. Krishnamurti*

There is one teacher–God himself. We are all pupils...
—*Hazrat Inayat Khan*

Teacher, teach thyself first. Lecturer, lecture to thyself first. Reformers, reform thyself first, Physician, heal thyself first...
—*Sivananda*

Thoughts

Thoughts are our enemy. When we are free of thoughts, we are naturally blissful. The gap between thoughts is our true state, it is the real Self. Get rid of thoughts, be empty of them, be in a state of perpetual thoughtlessness....
—*Ramana Maharshi*

If your thoughts are active, and your activities rushed, then you cannot be fully alive and conscious in the moment. Only if your thoughts are quiet and your heart at peace, can you be fully attentive and aware of the unfolding moment...

—*A Spiritual Warrior*

One's own thought is one's world. What a person thinks is what he becomes–That is the eternal mystery. If the mind dwells within the supreme Self, One enjoys undying happiness...

—*The Upanishads*

As soon as you have made a thought, laugh at it...—*Lao-tzu*

You are continuously radiating a mental energy which affects everything and everyone around you...

—*Annamalai Swami*

All that we are is the result of what we have thought; it is founded upon our thoughts, it is made up of our thoughts. If a man speaks or acts with an evil thought, pain follows him, as the wheel follows the foot of the ox that draws the carriage...If a man speaks or acts with a pure thought, happiness follows him, like a shadow that never leaves him...

—*Gautama Buddha*

Thoughts are there because you think...Thinking is not your nature. Your nature is unalloyed happiness...

—*Ramana Maharshi*

The power of thought is a mental dynamic of enormously powerful energy. It has been responsible for the soaring of humankind to the heights of achievement, and likewise for the sinking of man to the depths of degradation...

—*Shantidasa*

If we hold our thoughts on worldly, material things and refuse to think of that which is higher and subtler, then our faith in the Unseen will inevitably diminish...—*Paramananda*

The effect of living within a society oftentimes confuses and complicates our stream of thought. It makes people forget who they really are by causing them to be obsessed with what they are not... —*Lao-tzu*

If you don't catch...thoughts as they rise, they sprout, become plants and, if you still neglect them, they grow into great trees...If you can be so indifferent to it that it doesn't sprout or flourish, you are well on the way to escaping from the entanglements of the mind... —*Annamalai Swami*

If your thoughts center round the body, you will have worries about pains and illnesses, real or imaginary; if they are centered on riches, you will be worried about profit and loss, tax and exemptions, investment and insolvency; if they roam round fame, then you are bound to suffer from the ups and downs of scandal, calumny and jealousy...

—*Sathya Sai Baba*

Misery is due to the great multitude of discordant thoughts that prevail in the mind. If all thoughts be replaced by one single thought, there will be no misery...—*Ramana Maharshi*

Time

Time can be your joyous friends in the experience of spiritual being; or time can be your dreaded foe that dissolves illusions, breaks your attachments, and destroys your life...

— *A Spiritual Warrior*

One who is afraid of time becomes a prey of time. But time itself becomes a prey of that one who is not afraid of it...

—*Nisargadatta*

Time swallows up everything except character; this is the only thing it can not touch... —*Paramananda*

Let a man fix his mind on the reality and, having done this, he will transcend time... —*Mahabharata*

Time is your greatest advisor. Time will tell you if you can waste your life in illusion and fantasy thoughts, dwelling over past regrets, and future apprehensions. Just ask time, and time will point out that there are no survivors...

—*A Spiritual Warrior*

The timeless knows the time, the time does not know the timeless... —*Nisargadatta*

Truth

Truth does not reveal itself in the chatter of conversation, nor can it be coaxed to betray its secrets upon a printed page. Truth speaks only in the deep stillness of silence...

—*Shantidasa*

The Truth is one. The rest is illusion...Truth is betrayed by the first attempt at articulation... —*Yoga Swami*

Truth cannot be your monopoly: it is for the good of all...

—*Vivekananda*

If you seek the plain truth, be not concerned with right and wrong. The conflict between right and wrong is the sickness of the mind... —*Taoist saying*

"Be true to yourself" is the highest truth...—*A Spiritual Warrior*

The ritual of him who has seen the Truth is above anger and kindness, infidelity and religion... —*Rumi*

No truth remains as truth the moment it is given expression. It becomes a concept... —*Nisargadatta*

What is Truth? A difficult question; but I have solved it for myself by saying that it is what the "voice within" tells you...

—*Mohandas Gandhi*

If you want Truth as badly as a drowning man wants air, you will realize it in a split-second... —*The Upanishads*

Truth does not change; if truth were to change, truth would not be truth... —*Anonymous*

Truth will always triumph; do not doubt this in the least...
—*Sathya Sai Baba*

The name of God is Truth... —*Hindu saying*

Truth is never realized by the weak...—*Ramakrishnananda*

He who loves the Truth and subdues his whole being to the love of Truth shall find it... —*Bhagavad-Gita*

A man who seeks truth will never find it. Truth is in what IS and that is the beauty in it... —*Sunyata*

Never to have seen the truth is better than to have seen it and not acted upon it... —*Anonymous*

The plain truth is too simple for the seeker of complexity, who is looking for things he cannot understand...
—*Hazrat Inayat Khan*

There is no God higher than Truth... —*Mohandas Gandhi*

Truth is a diamond that scratches every other stone...
—*Shantidasa*

Though the sages speak in diverse ways, they express one and the same Truth... —*Srimad Bhagavatam*

We forget that Truth is self-sufficient and self-sustaining and does not require human hand to protect it...—*Paramananda*

Truth is not to be found by anybody who has not got an abundant sense of humility. If you would swim on the bosom of the ocean of Truth you must reduce yourself to zero...
—*Mohandas Gandhi*

War

Even fighting in self defense is wrong, though it is higher than fighting in aggression. There is no "righteous", indignation because indignation comes from not recognizing sameness in all things... —*Vivekananda*

Wealth

When you pile up riches, fear and anxiety are also piling up in proportion... —*Sathya Sai Baba*

The imperishable, inexhaustible wealth is the spiritual wealth. No thief can plunder this. He who has this wealth is the richest man...even if he is clad in rags, even if he has nothing to eat. He is the King of Kings. All other wealthy persons in the world are verily poor. They are beggars despite their material possessions... —*Sivananda*

Wealth and happiness do not dwell together. Rare is that wealthy man who does not have rivals and enemies who scandalize him... —*Yoga Vasistha*

A man's true wealth hereafter is the good he does in this world to his fellow-man... —*Mohammed*

A stingy person will always be poor, a generous person always rich... —*Anonymous*

Most rich people do not know how poor they really are... —*Shantidasa*

Even if one possessed the wealth of the whole world, but had no love for God, that man would be poor... —*Chidananda*

You are like a traveler who comes and goes. You accumulate wealth and take pride in your riches. But when you leave, you take nothing with you. You came into the world with your fists clenched, but when you go, your hands will be open... —*Kabir*

All amassing of wealth or hoarding of wealth above and beyond one's legitimate needs is theft... —*Mohandas Gandhi*

To try to extinguish the desire for riches with money is like trying to quench a fire with butterfat... —*Hindu saying*

The rich who only use their wealth for selfish purposes are sowing the seeds of eventual poverty. All that is not given is lost... —*Shantidasa*

The riches that you should strive to amass are not fields or factories, bungalows or bank balances, but wisdom and experience of oneness with the grandeur of the Universe and the force that runs it without a hitch... —*Sathya Sai Baba*

Wisdom

Wisdom is not gained by traveling afar, but by standing still; not by thought, but by the absense of thought...

—*Anonymous*

The sage has no creed of his own; and the reason is that he is egoless... —*Lakshmana Sarma*

Though a man be learned if he does not apply his knowledge, he resembles the blind man, who, lamp in hand, cannot see the road... —*Tibetan saying*

Wisdom gives praise liberally and makes promises discreetly...

—*Shantidasa*

The ignorant work for their own profit; the wise work for the welfare of the world... —*Bhagavad-Gita*

The way of the sage is to act but not compete...—*Leo Tolstoy*

Many men can utter words of wisdom, few men can practice it themselves... —*Hitopadesa*

By rousing himself, by earnestness, by restraint and control, the wise man makes for himself an island which no flood can immerse... —*Dhammapada*

The sage must distinguish between knowledge and wisdom. Knowledge is of things, acts and relations. But wisdom is of God alone; and, beyond all things, acts, and relations, it abides for ever. To become one with God is the only wisdom...

—*The Upanishads*

Wise company will make thee also wise... —*Sufi saying*

Wisdom is not in words, it is in understanding...

—*Hazrat Inayat Khan*

Wisdom does not attain completeness except through the living of life... —*Rabindranath Tagore*

It is knowledge that ultimately gives salvation...

—*Mohandas Gandhi*

The truly wise are anonymous; they do not display wisdom for the benefit or admiration of others... —*Anonymous*

Humility, unostentatiousness, non-injury, forgiveness, simplicity, purity, steadfastness, self-control; this is declared to be wisdom; what is opposed to this is ignorance...

—*Bhagavad-Gita*

The surest sign of a man of the highest wisdom is that he is unattracted by the pleasures of the world, for in him even the subtle tendencies have ceased. When these tendencies are strong, there is bondage; when they have ceased, there is liberation... —*Yoga Vasistha*

Wisdom does not rub off from one to another. Enlightenment is a do-it-yourself project... —*Shantidasa*

The falling drops of water will in time fill a water-jar. Even so the wise man becomes full of good, although he may gather in little by little... —*Dhammapada*

Wisdom is knowing which bridge to burn and which to cross over... —*Anonymous*

Words

When old words die out on the tongue, new melodies break forth from the heart... —*Rabindranath Tagore*

Because the truth cannot be accurately conveyed in words, it is pointless to query one man's opinion of the truth with another collection of words... —*Ramana Maharshi*

The six greatest words on earth are: "Control thyself!"—Cicero; "Know thyself!" —Socrates; "Give thyself!"–Jesus... —*Anonymous*

You should always keep your word. All the setbacks in life come only because you don't keep your word...—*Sivananda*

Monks and scholars should accept my word not out of respect, but upon analyzing it as a goldsmith analyzes gold, through cutting, melting and rubbing it...
—*Gautama Buddha*

Now if these words are helpful to you, put them into practice. But if they aren't helpful, then there's no need for them... —*Dalai Lama*

Words are but the shadows of thoughts and feelings...
—*Hazrat Inayat Khan*

The words of a man who practices austerity of speech cannot cause pain to others. His words will bring cheer and solace to others. His words will prove beneficial to all...
—*Sivananda*

One kind word has more power within it than a dozen ultimatums... —*Anonymous*

Our words are useless unless they come from the bottom of the heart... —*Mother Teresa*

Spiritual experience cannot be described in words. Language is imperfect... —*Sivananda*

Work

It is not what we do that has importance, but rather how well we do it... —*A Spiritual Warrior*

There is a criterion by which you can ascertain whether or not your work on earth is over. The criterion is: Are you still alive? If you are, there is still more work for you to do... —*Shantidasa*

If you wish to work properly, you should never lose sight of two great principles: first, a profound respect for the work undertaken, and second, a complete indifference to its fruits. Thus only can you work with the proper attitude... —*Brahmananda*

To work alone thou hast the right, but never the fruits thereof. Be thou neither actuated by the fruits of action, nor be thou attached to inaction... —*Bhagavad-Gita*

A vision without work is but a dream; a work without a vision is drudgery, alas; a vision and a work is the hope of the world... —*Anonymous*

Work of your own fee will, not from duty. We have no duty. The world is just a gymnasium in which we play; our life is an eternal holiday... —*Vivekananda*

Everyone has been made for some particular work, and the desire for that work has been put into his heart... —*Rumi*

In work, do what you enjoy... —*Lao-tzu*

It doesn't matter what you do as long as you do it with love... —*Mother Teresa*

While the unwise work for the fruit of their actions, the wise offer all results of their actions to Me... —*Bhagavad-Gita*

If you work at what you love to do you can't help but have love flowing through you... —*Shantidasa*

To live in the world or to leave it depends on the will of God. Therefore, work, leaving everything to Him. What else can you do?... —*Ramakrishna*

The surest sign of a person of the highest wisdom is that he or she is unattracted by the pleasures of the world...even the subtle tendencies have ceased... —*Yoga Vasistha*

Worry

Worry kills a man. It destroys his hope of life. It is a canker or cancer that slowly eats away at man. It wears you out. Do not worry over the past...Do not worry about things which are likely to happen; so often they really do not...—*Sivananda*

Mental problems feed on the attention you give them. The more you worry about them, the stronger they become. If you ignore them, they lose their power and finally vanish... —*Annamalai Swami*

There is nothing that wastes the body like worry, and one who has any faith in God should be ashamed to worry about anything whatsoever...—*Mohandas Gandhi*

When you worry about the problems of tomorrow, you are creating unhappiness for yourself today... —*Shantidasa*

To worry continually is the most efficient prayer for getting what you don't want... —*Shanidasa*

Worries do not belong to you. It is your own fault if you assume that they are yours... —*Ramana Maharshi*

Worry throws "faith in God" out the window...—*Anonymous*

One who has abandoned everything is not agitated by worry: if wind can sway the branches of a tree, it cannot be called immovable... —*Yoga Vasistha*

There is nothing to worry about. It is all God and His play. Clouds sweep over the sky : they appear and disappear; but the sky remains unaffected. So also the things of the world—its sorrows and its joys—they come and go: but we are eternal Changeless Existence, full of peace and bliss. We are the witness of a gigantic cinema show... —*Papa Ramdas*